"I didn't mean to [...] business…"

She held the doll out, and he stared for a second, then, looking disgusted, took it from her and carried it back to the counter. Unable to help herself, Callie added, "If your daughter really treasures it, maybe you could put it away for her."

Mark walked behind the counter and set the toy down.

"What do you think of her?"

His question caught her off guard. She tried to hush her mind so she could find something to say without throwing open a can of worms.

"I mean," Mark probed, "you didn't seem surprised. I assume you've always known."

She gave a sharp nod and panicked at the lump forming in her throat.

He waited, patient as always, forcing her to speak.

Callie choked the lump down and cleared her throat. "I heard about it after you moved back. I think she was a baby then."

"It must have surprised you."

She smiled faintly. "No, not that you had a family. I mean, it happens eventually."

Danielle Thorne is a Southern girl who treasures home and family. Besides books, she loves travel, history, cookies and naps. She's eternally thankful for the women she calls friends. Danielle is the author of over a dozen novels with elements of romance, adventure and faith. You'll often find her in the mountains or at the beach. She currently lives south of Atlanta with her sweetheart of thirty years and two cats.

Books by Danielle Thorne

Love Inspired

His Daughter's Prayer

Visit the Author Profile page at Harlequin.com.

His Daughter's Prayer

Danielle Thorne

LOVE INSPIRED
INSPIRATIONAL ROMANCE

LOVE INSPIRED®
INSPIRATIONAL ROMANCE

Recycling programs
for this product may
not exist in your area.

ISBN-13: 978-1-335-55376-8

His Daughter's Prayer

Copyright © 2020 by Danielle Thorne

This edition published by arrangement with Harlequin Books S.A.

For questions and comments about the quality of this book,
please contact us at CustomerService@Harlequin.com.

Love Inspired
22 Adelaide St. West, 40th Floor
Toronto, Ontario M5H 4E3, Canada
www.Harlequin.com

Printed in U.S.A.

And again, I will put my trust in him.
And again, Behold I and the children
which God hath given me.
—*Hebrews* 2:13

This story is dedicated to good men and fathers; to single dads, faithful husbands and stepfathers who fill empty shoes; and to all who walk beside little girls and boys until they can walk on their own. Thanks, Dad.

Chapter One

A brass bell jingled as Callie Hargrove strode into the Antique Market. She found the inside of the store as uninspiring as the simple name printed over the front window in block letters. The familiar fragrance of aged wood and furniture polish met her nose, and she inhaled to calm her nerves.

Looking around, she noted stacks of furniture and collectibles. It looked like they'd been plopped down as an afterthought. Not much had changed. She wondered if *he* had.

An old typewriter caught her attention, and she made her way over to it. Visiting the family business of her high school ex her first week back in town was unavoidable if she was going to impress her boss at her new temp job with the local real estate office here. With any luck, Mark Chatham wouldn't be around. She was here for hutches and old buffets that could be refinished and staged in model homes, not to be distracted by the fact that this was the Chatham family business.

She'd been gone awhile, working in Nashville, but it hadn't gotten her any closer to her dream of opening a boutique. With a job here this summer, she had a whole season to see if she could make a living here. If not, she'd head back to the city. Worries about seeing Mark again would have to wait.

Soft music drifted from the back of the store as Callie browsed. She knew both of the elderly Chathams had passed away, so the new manager must be busy in the back. Not that Ragland, Georgia, had a high crime rate, but some people still knew the value of things covered in dust. She certainly did, and she needed the inventory for the boutique she wanted to make happen here. If not, it was back to Nashville and the urban grind.

Callie scanned the faded oyster-colored walls, and her mouth fell open. Behind the checkout counter hung a display rack with the most beautiful spoons she'd ever seen. They shimmered like a beacon. They were handsome, engraved silverware from decades or centuries past. She tripped over a wooden rocking horse in her hurry to study them.

Her mind raced with ideas. They'd look amazing on a freshly painted wall. They'd look amazing on her own walls. Forgetting about staging homes for the local real estate company, she wondered if she could buy the spoons for herself, split them up and sell them. It'd be enough to settle her credit card debts and open her own shop.

She slipped behind the counter, stood on her tiptoes and ran a finger along the edge of the spoon rack. It was buffed to a high sheen, one of the few things that didn't appear to be coated in dust.

"Can I help you?"

Callie jumped, even as the quiet, familiar timbre made her heart stand still. She turned, hoping to see a crotchety old employee, the kind who acted like they didn't really want to rid themselves of surplus junk piled to the ceilings.

No such luck. Her heart liquefied and sluiced down into her gut.

The man who'd walked up behind her was not old, although crotchety was a possibility. Mark Chatham looked almost exactly as she remembered him, only better if that were possible—taller, filled out and with crinkles around his brilliant eyes. A slight trembling in her hands made her fold them into loose fists.

"Those aren't for sale."

She forced a smile, as she struggled for something to say. "I, uh…" Callie glanced over her shoulder at the wall. "I really like the spoon set. They're beautiful."

He studied her for a long while like he couldn't believe what he was seeing. "They are," he said at last. "They were my grandmother's, so I'm sorry, but they're not for sale."

Callie reminded herself—this was work. Strictly business. She had a boutique she planned to open. "Everything's for sale." She lifted the corner of her mouth teasingly.

"Not these, Callie." Mark took a step forward, shrinking the space between them, and she realized he could trap her behind the counter if he wanted. They could pick up their argument right where they'd left off over ten years ago. To her relief, he held out a hand instead.

"How are you? Your sister told me you were moving back to Ragland."

For some reason, Callie couldn't bring herself to reach out and touch the hand of her first serious crush. Was this really the boy who'd given her her first kiss?

She reached into her purse for a business card. "Yes, I'm back home for now. I'm working with Martin Hometown Realty, staging homes for the summer."

"Is that so?" Mark motioned to the store.

"Well, welcome back. I have lots of pieces around here that don't need much work, and they're fine quality."

After handing him her card, Callie folded her arms to hide the fact that the sound of his voice was making her tremble. She tried to focus on what she wanted. The antique spoon collection.

Even though he'd refused, an imaginary billboard with dancing flatware in the back of her head chanted, *Spoons! Spoons! Spoons!* She narrowed her eyes, tried to look apologetic and gave him her most bashful smile. "It's really good to see you again, but I need those spoons, Mark. How about fifteen hundred dollars?"

He shook his head again. "Nope." Something about his tone reminded her of the day he'd refused to try to work things out between them. And then he'd run off.

She swallowed and stood up straight. She could be all business, too. "No counteroffer?"

"Nope," he repeated. He glanced past her at the spoon rack and put his hands on his hips. "I'm sorry," he said. "It's nice to see you again. Have a look around and let me know if there's anything else you'd like."

He dropped his arms and walked off. Dismissed. Just like at the end of his senior year. Well, she was more stubborn now, too. "Why do you have them on the wall if they're not for sale?"

He didn't reply. Instead, he disappeared past a narrow grandfather clock into the back.

She furrowed her brows. Why wasn't the clock against the wall? It looked like he just dropped stuff wherever there was an empty space.

Frustrated, she pursed her lips. Yes, she'd come in search of a sideboard or curio cabinet to refinish, but those silver heirlooms would bring in top dollar even if she sold them individually. She could even put them away and wait until she was out of debt and ready to open her place.

The spoons gleamed in the sunshine. Dust particles whirled in a shaft of light. Country music echoed from a radio. Callie turned on her heel. Everything had its price. Mark Chatham should know that; he'd sold out and moved to Florida after dumping her and his baseball career.

She picked her way past the shop's odds and ends until she reached a cleared aisle. Then she marched toward the back of the store, calculating how irresponsible it would be to use all of her emergency savings and max out her credit cards on a set of a dozen spoons. She couldn't help herself. Everything was negotiable—even with old boyfriends.

Callie passed under an ancient green exit sign. A door on the left stood open. She wrinkled her nose to stave off a sneeze. A rustling of papers in the room drew her over to the door.

Mark jerked when she moved into the doorway. "Did you find something else?" he asked.

Callie couldn't resist teasing him. "Actually, I sell refinished furniture on the side, too, and I'm good at it."

"Great," he said before she could finish. "What would you like to see?"

A glimmer of humor sparkled in his eyes. His unruffled demeanor made her feel like he was an older, wiser bird, and she was nothing more than an amusing little parakeet. Behind him, she noticed a framed picture of a baby girl wearing pink-and-white ruffles. Her heart flopped to the ground this time. It was the daughter. She'd heard about her. Callie grimaced inside and out.

"How about two thousand dollars?" She dropped her smile and put on her best *I mean business* face. "For old times' sake? It'd certainly motivate me to come back when I need other things for staging."

Mark stood up with a spreadsheet in his hand, and the sparkle in his eyes clouded over with something else. "The spoons aren't for sale, and I'm closing up for lunch in a few minutes so you may want to finish looking."

His tone hurt. He wasn't impressed that she'd moved back home, and he wasn't interested in her offer. The natural charm she'd relied on since she was a little girl with dimples had no effect on him anymore.

Was he married? she wondered. No one had told her. Oh, yes, she'd heard he was a single dad. So now he didn't even blink when a woman walked into his store alone? That made him as rare as his spoons.

She realized he was waiting for some kind of answer. Glancing at his hand and seeing no wedding band, Callie's mouth turned up at the corners. "I'll finish up front by myself then," she said, calculating how long she should wait to come back. It wouldn't make sense not to return with the store so close by.

"Okay." He sat back down in his chair and picked up a pair of frameless glasses.

Dismissed. Again. Usually, Callie had to find a way to extricate herself from conversations with men. Most people seemed to find her interesting or funny. Mark acted like she was another piece of furniture, not a girl he'd dated for over two years. The picture of the baby on his desk pricked her heart again. He'd found someone better, right after high school. She was old news, even if it hadn't worked out for him.

Callie returned to the front of the store. Irritated with her experience seeing Mark for the first time in years, she decided not to look around anymore. Maybe she'd come back the day after tomorrow. There'd probably be another employee here.

She glanced at the clock on her phone as she hurried out the door. It was time for lunch. Shoving down the unease seeing Mark had caused, she swallowed hard and hit the sidewalk, making her way past a salon and an abandoned shop on the corner. At least seeing Mark for the first time was over. Done. They had run into each other and acted civil. He had his shop and a daughter. She had her career.

She wiped her damp palms on her slacks and took a deep breath of floral summer air. It filled her with hope. Her favorite diner was still open on the square, and she hoped they still sold her favorite burgers.

Just before closing for the day, Mark shook hands with Mrs. Bake, relieved she'd taken the 1950s buffet off his hands. Midcentury antiques were becoming popular, and he'd had the piece for over a year. He'd bet it'd look fantastic in her home, not that he'd been inside, but he knew she ran the classiest floral shop in the county.

With the store quiet again and the lunch crowd rush gone, he strolled back to the office, his mind whirling over Callie Hargrove. Seeing her again had taken his breath away the moment she'd looked over at him. Her wavy, mahogany-colored hair had a copper shine to it, and those eyes of hers were still a spectacular brown that gleamed like brass.

He'd never forgotten her. Although he'd heard she might be back in Ragland, it had taken him by surprise when she strode in, so much so that he could only stare and robotically tell her that the spoons weren't for sale. He never dreamed she'd come into his shop.

Mark blinked to keep his feelings in check as memories assaulted him. The last time they were together, they'd been standing on the base-ball practice field, arguing about their plans for the future. He'd decided to join the Coast Guard no matter what she—or his parents or the town—thought. She couldn't convince him to accept the offer from Nashville's minor league baseball team. He knew she had dreams of going to design school there, but he didn't want to play baseball. Their lives were going in different directions.

She still looked gorgeous, and her interest in the spoons was charming. People asked about them often, but he couldn't let go of his family's beloved heirlooms passed down through many happy marriages, even though he suspected that finding a "love of his life" might not be in the stars for him. Callie was the only girl who'd ever come close. Regardless, some kind of odd hope—or maybe it was faith—compelled him to hang on to them and keep them in a place where he could see them every day.

The old rotary phone in the office rang, and he headed toward it and scooped up the receiver.

"Antique Market."

"Hey, Mark, this is Robby from Community Trust Bank."

Mark's stomach roiled. He forced words to come out of his mouth. "Afternoon, Robby, what can I do for you?"

"Hate to bother you, Mark, but we had our quarterly meeting today, and the top brass is asking about your note."

Mark swallowed. "Did they now." Robby's boss, Matt McIntyre, operated a tiny county bank, but he fought the urge to say so. "What'd you tell him?"

"Oh, just that we talked last month, and you need another few weeks to catch up."

"That's right," Mark agreed. "I put something in the mail this morning, but I'm still short for May. April's caught up, though, right?"

The sound of keyboard clicks came through the phone. Mark let out a slow breath to calm his thumping heart. Frustrated with his grandparents for not buying the place outright, he twisted the phone cord in his hand.

"Yes, we're good for April," came Robby's response. "If May is coming, then I'll let him know we're just a couple weeks behind. Should be caught up by next quarter, right?"

"That's right."

"Good deal then, Chatham." Robby dropped the business act and flipped to neighborly. "Are you going to the game on Saturday?"

"Yes, I'll be there," Mark assured him. "Wouldn't miss it for the world."

"See you there, player."

Robby hung up, and Mark put the phone down with a shake of his head. He walked around the desk and folded himself into the old swivel chair. He'd brought a microwave burrito for lunch, but he wasn't in the mood to warm it up. Grabbing a can of honey-roasted peanuts from his stash he tossed some into his mouth. Then he propped his legs up on the desk.

The rent on the building was almost caught up for May and then he had this month to deal with. July lurked just around the corner. It was the first time he'd ever fallen behind like this; there'd always been extra acreage from the family farm to sell off the last time business was slow. But he'd reached the limits of what he was comfortable parting with.

Home was safety and peace. Plus, it was paid for. The store was… Well, it was the Chatham legacy, and he would pass it on to his daughter, Hadley. Hopefully. If he didn't lose it. He just had to find a way to hold off the bank and increase the shop's sales. He was confident he'd pull through.

Speaking of confidence, Callie Hargrove had no shortage of that. She'd known exactly what she was doing, grinning at him like that and offering him good money for the spoons—but it wasn't enough.

The phone rang again, and he glanced at his watch. It would be time to pick up Hadley from pre-K soon. He leaned over to answer the phone. Regrets or not, that was the only girl he'd ever let charm him again.

Callie stopped at the diner on Ragland's town square where she'd eaten while growing up. It still had a dreadful name, Grub 'n' Go, but the food was delicious.

She ordered a Reuben sandwich and splurged on a bowl of triple chocolate ice cream. With Mark haunting her mind, she studied the spoon in her hand. It was nowhere near as beautiful as the spoons on his shop's wall.

She hated being broke, but the passion for turning old things into new was an expensive hobby. Someday, it'd be a career, and she'd have her own boutique, but first she had to come up with a way to get out of debt and save up more money.

She'd failed to open up her own place in Nashville because she found herself living paycheck to paycheck and running up credit card debts, but she wasn't ready to give up on her dream yet. This summer in Ragland was her last chance. With the job staging furniture, she could work on finding a way to open her own boutique in town. If that didn't work she'd head back to Nashville and find another job with an interior design company like she'd done for years, but at least her family couldn't say she hadn't given Ragland a second chance. Her sister, Amanda, had been begging her to move home for years. She worked for the real estate company as an agent, and had helped Callie get the staging job.

She gave Gabby a small wave as she slipped out the front door. The Grub 'n' Go cashier was the daughter of one of her old friends. She'd welcomed her back with a hug and said nothing about Mark. Nobody had. Callie had told her about her new job while waiting on the burger.

She was working for Martin Hometown Realty, located inside an old restored train station around the corner. It felt odd to drive just a couple short blocks to get everywhere she needed to go, but Ragland was that small. Even the grocery store was just a mile from her little cottage summer rental, which was a fast bike ride if she could fit everything into a basket. She added *Buy a bicycle* to her mental shopping list as she drove over to the realty office.

Callie skipped inside with excitement. The owner, Brett Martin, stood in the lobby in nice slacks and a flashy watch.

"Callie," he called. He beamed at her and held his palm out for a handshake.

"Hi, boss." She shook his hand happily.

"You're going to do great here." He shook her hand and motioned toward the small office he'd promised her that she'd already set up. "The computer is in, and you're ready to go."

"That's amazing." All Callie had at home was a cheap laptop. Having the office provide a real computer and fast Wi-Fi would be a relief. "I stopped at the antiques store on the square," she added. "I didn't pick anything up, but we're just getting started."

He pointed across the room. "After what you did with that bench over there, I can't wait to see what you do next. We have a whole shed of furniture that needs help."

"I'll have a look this weekend," Callie said. "I'm not sure what I can do with 1980s hotel furniture by the end of the summer, but a few nips and tucks will be a start."

"I'm glad that you can do upholstery, too," Mr. Martin said. "I was so impressed with the bench, I had it put in the lobby."

"That's great. I don't have room for it at home, and I don't have a listing that's ready for it yet, either." She grinned up at him. "Thanks for the office. I've never had my own before, just a cubicle."

"Well, get to work, Picasso, because I have two new houses ready to go on the market, and they need help."

Callie laughed and saluted him, then hurried to the back. Amanda and her husband had helped move in some books, folder files, framed pictures and whiteboards the day before.

This job had been Amanda's idea. The office needed a temporary home stager, so Callie had moved back and would take the opportunity to see if she could open her dream boutique here.

Grateful Mr. Martin had welcomed her help for the summer, Callie sighed with happiness as she pushed open the door to her office. Once she hung up a few decorations and calendars, the fern-colored walls would calm her nerves, and the enormous window would let in sunlight, even if it only provided a view of the parking lot.

She'd hit the flea markets this weekend.

Maybe she'd find some nice candlestick holders or colorful vases.

She thought of the spoons in Mark's shop and frowned. She needed them. The question was, how could she convince the handsome proprietor to let them go?

Chapter Two

Mark glanced back to make sure he'd parked the truck straight. Every Saturday, busy moms whipped in like race-car drivers in between the softball games, and sometimes he found himself blocked in. Grabbing his favorite bats from the truck bed, he reached for Hadley's hand, hopped over the curb and made a beeline for field three.

"I played with a ball at school yesterday."

He looked down at Hadley's mussed hair half out of its ponytail and squeezed her hand. "Did you hit it real hard like Daddy?"

She tilted her head back and gazed up into his eyes with pride. "No, I threw it at Logan and hit him in the head."

Mark frowned. "You shouldn't throw balls at people, Hadley."

"He's mean." Her response came out a stubborn whine.

Mark brushed his thumb over her hand as they marched toward the ball field. There was no use arguing with a five-year-old. If he didn't make her cry, he'd spawn a thousand questions all starting with "why?"

It'd been a mistake to keep her home or with their family friend, Lois, all these years instead of putting her in day care. Her socialization had been hit or miss. This pre-K program was a last-ditch attempt to get her ready for kindergarten by fall. She was only two months in at Little Steps Academy and already turning the place upside down with her curiosity and impulsiveness. Not to mention, her inability get along with anyone.

"How about I get you a hot dog to eat while you watch Daddy play?"

Today his softball team, the Copperheads, played the Hornets from the next county over, and he wanted a win.

Marching to the concession stand, he pacified Hadley with a plain hot dog and bag of potato chips. He hoped Lois would get to the ball field in time to sit with her before the game started. He planted Hadley on the dugout bench with her food and a warning to stay put, but she made him say a blessing over her lunch like she did with Lois before he left. With a sigh, he hurried out onto the field.

"Goldie!"

Someone called out his childhood nickname, and Mark lifted his chin to acknowledge it. Several of his teammates were already on the field in their white-and-gold jerseys, tossing balls. He dropped his bag and bats and ran out onto the field.

"Hey, second baseman!" Todd shouted again.

Mark returned Todd's salute and headed for him in the outfield to warm up. His friend raised a ball like a question, and Mark nodded. He raised his glove and caught a hard throw that Todd tried to catch him off guard with. They both laughed.

"Who's minding the store?" Todd shouted. *Smack.* He jumped aside but caught Mark's ball.

"Lois. She's closing up for a while to come watch Hadley, though." Mark wondered if he should mention Callie had come by. She was Todd's sister-in-law after all, but he decided against it. Word would get around soon.

Todd grinned. He wound up and threw a fastball.

Mark had to jump to catch it. "You throw like a girl," he called.

Todd yelled back, "Nothing to be ashamed of. My wife can outpitch me."

"Family affair," Mark laughed. He knew

Amanda played, and one of their kids was into T-ball. In a year or two, he hoped Hadley might give it a try, but right now she could barely stand still long enough to brush her teeth.

The ump blew a few short trills on the whistle to gather everyone up. The Hornets would bat first.

Mark hurried back to check on Hadley, who'd dropped her food in the dirt. After drying her tears and showing her only the bun was ruined and she could still eat the hot dog, he jogged back out and took up his position on second base.

Turning twenty-eight had been a surprise for him. He realized the years would keep coming, and he could do nothing to stop them; worse, he had no one at his side to watch them go by with. Playing softball kept him active in the community. It was good for his and Hadley's social life and nice for business, too. People seemed to have forgotten their disappointment when he didn't go into the minor leagues after high school. No one said much about it—or about him being a single father. At least to his face.

For a second, his gaze went to the dugout, and he saw Hadley trying to push the end of a bat through one of the holes in the fence.

He turned his attention to the game and waited for the batter to hit the ball. "Let's go!"

Daylight shone through the sunroof as Callie tapped her nails on the steering wheel. It made her think about Amanda and the times they'd helped each other get dressed for proms and school dances. They were only three years apart, but sometimes it felt like centuries.

Her older sister was her mentor and best friend. They didn't always get along or agree, but Amanda was always there and more patient with Callie than their mother had been. After Callie's mother passed, her father lived in their family home alone, but Callie had stayed in Nashville. It'd been Amanda who'd convinced Callie to come home for a while now and work on opening a boutique.

Callie had already inquired about the empty store on the square. It was out of her price range, but if she approached the bank again with a strong bid, maybe they'd agree to loan her the money. She wondered what Mark would think of her being a few shops down from him.

Pushing the thought away, Callie noticed the sign for the ballpark. *Eureka!* She could drop off her treasures from the early-morning flea market at her house later. Todd had a ball game today, and that meant grilled hot dogs, hamburgers, sunshine and company. Forget working on the weekend. She needed a break after the big move.

The parking lot looked packed. Summer sports were a thing in Ragland. Todd, Amanda and their oldest, Justin, all played. Little Nicole was too young, but they'd have her playing T-ball in no time.

Easing the car into a spot far from the action, Callie flipped off the engine and hurried across the parking lot while texting her sister about which field Todd was playing on.

Field Three came the reply.

Callie snaked her way through the crowd, inhaling the smell of grilled hamburgers with mouthwatering excitement. She may have pretended to enjoy five-star dining occasionally, but she loved concession stand food.

The sun was hot by the time she reached the metal bleachers. She stepped up the first stair and turned to see if she could spot Todd on the field in his Copperheads jersey.

She scanned the athletes until her eyes stopped on the second baseman. He looked familiar. Gorgeous blond hair peeked out from underneath his baseball cap. His tanned hand smacked the glove, and he called something out to the shortstop. Callie squinted. It was Mark Chatham.

She took another step up the bleachers, almost tripping as she twisted around to keep her eyes on second base. Yes, it was him.

"Callie! Over here!"

Amanda's voice captured her attention, and Callie climbed up to where her sister sat with her kids. Beautiful, sweet Justin had a red toy car in his hand. Nicole sat subdued in her mother's lap, sucking a lollipop.

Amanda patted the bench beside her, and Callie sat down. "I thought you were headed to Taylorsville?"

"I hit the flea markets early this morning, and I found a few things I can use for the office."

"Any spoons?" her sister teased.

"No. I shouldn't have told you about that if you're going to tease me, and by the way, you could have told me Mark was on the team."

Amanda looked chagrined. "Sorry. I honestly didn't think about it. I was worried about you getting settled."

"I'm settled enough except for transporting furniture." Callie pretended to shrug off the fact her high school sweetheart was a hundred yards away. She struggled to focus on her current problems instead. "I'm going to need Todd's truck from now on when I pick things up, because I can't fit anything bigger than a magazine rack in my car."

"Sure, no problem."

Callie glanced at her sister and twisted her lips into a smirk. "Don't worry, I'll ask him. It'd only be on Saturdays once in a while."

Amanda nodded. "You can always have them hold stuff for you, and we can pick up later."

"That's what I did in Nashville, but this is different. I don't have a showroom truck to pick up things for me, and places out here are farther apart."

Amanda patted her leg. "Don't worry. Someone will help you out. Do you want to get sticky? I have an extra lollipop."

"Nope." Everyone in the stands cheered, and Callie turned her attention back to the game. Mark caught a line drive that would have taken his head off if he'd missed. "Wow, good catch!" she blurted.

Amanda jumped to her feet. "Way to go, Chatham!" She hooted like a teenager.

He glanced their way, and Callie blushed. "Do you mind?" she asked. The people around them laughed.

"If you come to the games you have to cheer," Amanda cried with glee. She stood up again and shouted at her husband on the pitcher's mound. "Come on, baby, strike this guy out!"

Callie laughed under her breath. Todd threw a big grin Amanda's way. Sometimes they acted like they were still newlyweds. She glanced at Mark intently watching the batter, and ignored the flickering sensation in her heart.

She shook her head as her stomach growled. "I'm going to get something to eat," she said.

Justin jumped to his feet, waving his toy in the air. "Take me with you, Aunt Callie!"

She smiled and held her arms out, and he dashed past his mother to his aunt. Laughing, she swung him around, and the crowd roared again. She set him down and looked. Someone in the outfield had caught a fly ball, and the teams were switching out. She hurried to the concession stand with Justin and made it back before Todd was up at bat.

Munching on her hamburger, Callie managed to cheer alongside Amanda until out of the corner of her eye, she noticed a tall, older woman with gray-streaked hair at the Copperheads' dugout. She was speaking with great animation to a little girl who stomped out of the dugout and followed the woman toward the bleachers. They sat on the bottom row, the child chattering about something and kicking her legs in the air.

Callie elbowed Amanda in the ribs. "Who's that little girl?"

Amanda glanced down. "That's his daughter."

For a moment, Callie couldn't speak. The little ragamuffin had tangled, dirty blond hair, darker than her father's. She squirmed on the seat beside her unfamiliar caretaker. A daughter. Mark had given Callie up for a life in Florida and met someone else. Someone else he'd loved enough to have a family with.

"So, where's the rest of the family?" she asked.

"Oh, they're—" Distracted, Amanda glanced toward the bleachers across the field. "His parents used to come to all of the games," she said, "even in high school."

"Yes, I remember. I know they're gone, but I meant, doesn't he have any cousins or somebody around anymore?"

"Not that I know of." Amanda glanced at their neighbors to make sure no one eavesdropped. She leaned in closer. "That woman sitting with his daughter works at the Antique Market sometimes, and I think she's his babysitter. I don't remember her name."

"Did his mother ever know her?"

"Yes, but she didn't know her long. Mrs. Chatham passed away like three or four years ago. His dad died just a couple years after high school, remember?"

"Yes." Callie kept her gaze on the field like they were just having a casual conversation. "So, Todd and Mark are still close friends?"

Amanda looked at her with undisguised curiosity. "Yeah, they still hang out a little. They started again when Mark moved back after we got married."

This caught Callie's attention. "But he didn't come to the wedding."

Amanda frowned. "That's ancient history. He didn't want to make you uncomfortable, and he had other commitments."

Like a baby, thought Callie. Instead she said, "I'm just surprised he didn't come when he was asked to be a groomsman."

"Todd understood. Besides, you had a hot date, and I didn't want to upset my favorite bridesmaid."

"Oh, no," Callie said, shaking her head. "I wouldn't have minded. We were ancient history by then."

"Right," Amanda said with a smile. "And now?"

"I just want his antique spoons." They broke into chuckles.

Suddenly a bat made a cracking sound, and she jumped up to cheer with everyone else. One of the Copperheads had hit a ball over the fence. Everyone jumped up and down on the bleachers until they shook.

Callie settled back into her seat, glancing down at the little girl sliding on and off the bottom bleacher shouting a children's nursery rhyme while the woman beside her shushed her. It diverted Callie's attention back to Mark. He was focused, serious, sturdy.

Callie looked away. The air felt hot and the seats were hard, but the food tasted good and the game was fun. She hadn't been to a softball game since she'd left home. She took a deep breath and studied the scoreboard.

It wasn't the mall or the market district in Nashville; it wasn't a coffee shop or hanging out with her coworkers at an interior design studio. But that was okay. Amanda was here, people were nice and she had a job. It almost felt like home again.

She sneaked a glance down at Mark's daughter. Almost.

The Hornets caught up in the third inning, but the Copperheads eventually won the game. It was hot and humid by the end of the ninth inning, and Lois's husband, the team shortstop, was sprawled across the dugout bench like a beached whale.

"Ridley," Mark said, as he reached for his bag.

"Good game, my man," Ridley said from the bench.

"Are you going to be okay?"

"These noon Saturday games are a killer. They got to move us to after dinner."

Mark chuckled. "Next week is four-thirty."

"Music to my ears," Ridley muttered.

"Daddy!"

Mark turned around in time to catch Hadley diving into his arms. He caught her as Ridley sat up and straightened his jersey.

"Hi, Mr. Ridley." Then she pointed at the dugout door, and Mark watched Lois approach with her hands on her hips.

"I told her to wait with me," Lois said, frowning at Hadley.

Hadley buried her head in Mark's sweaty shirt. He set her down on the bench, and Ridley smiled at her. "You came to see me, didn't you?"

"No." Hadley grinned.

Lois stepped inside and hauled her husband up by the shoulder. "We have things to do, and by things, I mean you need to mow the lawn."

Ridley groaned.

"Thanks for going back to the store, Lois," Mark called to her.

"It's no problem," she said before her husband could complain. She shook her finger at Hadley. "You be good for your daddy today, or I'm going to make you sweep the shop floor."

Hadley frowned and folded her arms. Mark

laughed, thanked Lois for watching his baby girl on top of minding the store on Saturday then led Hadley out by her sticky hand to make room for the other players to get their things.

"Goldie!" Todd hollered as Mark headed off the field with his bag slung over his shoulder.

Mark nodded at his friend. "Great game."

"You, too. That puts us up back on top even though it was close."

Mark shrugged. "We'll probably see them again in the playoffs."

Todd pumped his fist. "And we'll be ready."

Mark laughed as Todd's wife approached him, pulling their own kids behind her. Justin held hands with another woman. His heart did a swan dive. Callie Hargrove.

He couldn't mistake the strong face and easy smile. The smile that slid off her face when she saw him looking at her.

"Good game, babe!" shouted Amanda. She jumped into Todd's arms and planted a kiss on his lips. Their little girl shouted, "Daddy!" and grabbed a leg. Callie and the little boy just watched.

Mark's mind swirled for something to say.

Amanda broke the ice. "Great hit out there today, Goldie. And two catches!"

"You keeping score?" he joked.

She tapped her forehead. "Oh," she said, like

she'd just recalled something, "you know Callie's back, right?" She motioned toward her, and Callie slid the aviator-style sunglasses off her face. She stared at him, and he wondered if he had dirt on his chin, then he remembered Hadley weaving in and out of his legs.

"You remember Mark," Amanda stated, like they hadn't seen each other in a century.

"Yes, I know. Hi, again," Callie spoke at last. Maybe she wasn't upset with him over the spoons, but the past was another question.

"We saw each other the other day," Mark said.

"At the Antique Market, yes."

Feeling Amanda and Todd watching the exchange, Mark nodded. Surely Callie had told her sister she'd waltzed into the Market and tried to buy his family heirlooms.

An awkward pause settled around them. Mark made himself act casual. He was tired, but seeing her again sparked something inside of him he hadn't felt in a long time. His mind raced for something more to say.

Hadley took care of things for him. She looked up at Callie while wiping her nose with a dirty hand. "Who are you?"

Mark froze.

"This is my sister, Callie," Amanda interjected. She pointed at her son. "Callie is Justin's aunt."

Hadley glanced at Justin, whom she played with on a few occasions, then turned her attention back to Callie. "You're not an ant."

Callie evidently put it together. "I'm an aunt, not an ant," she tried to explain.

Hadley wrinkled her brows, then pulled away from her father and skipped over to Justin. "Do you eat bugs?"

Mark tried to plaster a polite smile on his face and turned back to the adults.

"I didn't know you still played." Callie motioned toward the field.

"Um, yeah, just for fun now."

"Oh, you should see him, Cal," Todd said. "He's the best. Took us all the way to the playoffs two years in a row."

Mark waved him off. "Says the pitcher."

Todd grinned, then looked at Callie. "Didn't you two date in high school?"

Callie was speechless. Amanda tilted her head at Todd, then punched him on the shoulder.

Mark shuffled his feet. "Nice to see you again," he said to Callie as he hitched the bag strap over his shoulder.

Callie must have felt mortified, too, because she blurted out, "So, did you change your mind yet?"

He knew exactly what she was referring to. She wasn't the type to let things go. "No."

She chuckled at his brusque answer. "Are you sure you even know what I'm talking about?"

He felt a tug at the corner of his mouth at the look in her eyes. The blinding afternoon sun made her eyes appear brighter than they had in the shop. Her skin was naturally tan.

"I meant the spoons," she said.

"They're still not for sale." He let himself smile. There was no use in keeping his amusement from her at this point. If she wanted to play a game, that was fine. He'd play, but only because she was cute; he'd never sell them. Not ever.

"Like I told you," he said, glancing toward the parking lot as the crowd around them thinned, "just about everything in the store is for sale but not the spoons."

"You must have been very close to your grandma," teased Callie.

He lifted a brow. "Something like that."

Todd watched the exchange with interest. "What spoons?"

Amanda laughed, grabbed his hand and yelled at Justin to get out of the dirt. Hadley was right there with him.

"Bye, Goldie. Stay out of trouble!" called Amanda, dragging her crew away.

Mark waved and turned his attention back to

Callie. She was studying him, but when he caught her doing it, she put her sunglasses back on.

"I may come by again this week," she warned.

"If I'm not there, Lois will be."

Callie raised a brow. "Your manager?" She sounded hopeful.

"No," he smiled again. "She worked for my parents for decades, and now she works for me."

Mark thought he detected a glimmer of disappointment behind the shades. Pulling the bag strap back over his shoulder again, he took the opportunity to walk off with the last word. "She won't sell you the spoons, either."

A gurgle of laughter echoed behind him as he walked away to fetch his daughter in the dirt and head home.

Ragland's countryside flew by out the truck window as he headed home with Hadley tucked in behind him in her booster seat.

He couldn't recall when he'd first decided to break it off with Callie, but he'd known he would leave town after graduating and there had been no use stringing her along. She'd taken it pretty hard. His regrets came later. He'd missed her so much, but by then she'd gone to Nashville.

"Daddy, turn the music on."

"We're almost home."

"But I want to sing."

Mark started her favorite CD, then pulled off the road into his driveway with a sigh. He jumped out to grab the mail. Climbing back into the truck, he rattled along the gravel until they came up to the house.

The Chatham house was a brick ranch surrounded by azalea bushes. An older home down the road with a sweeping lawn built by his grandparents had been sold after they passed. At the more recent house where Mark had grown up, only a small swatch of grass in the front acted as a proper yard.

The place was surrounded by fields that needed cutting a couple times in the summer. Sometimes, he rented out the land to a few friends who liked to hunt in the fall. But now with most of the land sold off, there wasn't much left to deal with.

The brakes squeaked as he came to a stop and killed the engine. Tired but satisfied that the Hornets had been beaten well enough to stop the jokes for a while, Mark headed inside. Hadley followed close behind.

He threw the mail and his keys onto the counter, then grabbed a water bottle out of the fridge. "Here," he said, following Hadley into the living room. She turned on the television. "Drink this," he said firmly.

She accepted it but pointed at the screen. "I want to watch."

"You need a bath."

"But I want to watch."

Guilt hit him in the chest. She'd already sat through his softball game. "Okay," he relented, "but stay right here. I'm going to wash up."

"Okay."

"Be a good girl."

Silence.

Kicking off his shoes, Mark passed a picture of his great-grandfather dressed in a dark blue military uniform, and his mind drifted back to the spoons.

They were symbols of love and sacrifice, something Callie would love even more if she knew the whole story. He suspected Amanda had talked her into moving home to Ragland, but why move back to an old town in the middle of nowhere Georgia to work for a mom-and-pop business like Martin Hometown Realty? He imagined her working in Atlanta or Birmingham, not Ragland.

She'd always been creative. Staging homes seemed right up her alley. She'd mentioned flipping furniture, too, but that wasn't much of a living, not without a shop. No wonder she had to take the real estate job.

The home phone rang. It kept jangling so he

hurried back into the kitchen and picked up the receiver. "Hello?"

"Mark?" Lois sounded like she was out of breath. "We have a problem."

Mark closed his eyes. "What's the matter?"

"I think we have a busted pipe in the Market. Water's dripping down from the ceiling tiles in the corner over the hutch we moved last month."

Mark sighed. "Call Jake," he advised, then assured her that while she called their plumber he was on his way. He hurried back out to the living room. Hadley was nodding off on the couch.

"I'm sorry, honey," he whispered, trying to pick her up.

"Don't!"

"Daddy has to go to work."

"No!" Her eyes filled with tears. "I want to watch the cartoons."

"I'm sorry, but we have to go."

She screamed, "I want to stay here!" but he picked her up anyway and carried her on his shoulder. Grabbing his shoes he'd kicked off at the door, Mark hurried back out to the truck, trying to stay calm while Hadley tried to get out of his arms.

After buckling Hadley back into her booster against her will, Mark cranked up her music to appease her as he hurried back to town, even singing along with her to make her happy. All the while, his mind raced. Leaks and water damage. Great. He'd have to use his insurance if they'd cover it. He didn't have extra money to be throwing away on repairs, not with the bank pressuring him about his late payments. He pushed aside persistent thoughts of Hadley's troublesome behavior and the fact that Callie was back in town.

He had a livelihood to worry about.

Chapter Three

A slammed door woke Callie with a start. She sat straight up in bed, her senses on high alert. Footsteps sounded across the living room floor of her new place just a few blocks from the office, and her heart pounded.

"Callie?"

Her shoulders slumped in relief. She flung off the covers and jumped out of bed. Bright sunlight streamed through the window. It looked like she'd slept in this Sunday morning.

"Callie? Are you here?"

Callie skipped across the floor and down the hall. Seeing her sister, she put her hands on her hips. "Amanda, what are you doing walking in and scaring me to death like that?"

Amanda laughed. She looked like she'd already run a million errands. "What are you doing sleeping until noon?"

"I was tired. It's been a long first week."

Amanda looked around. "I see you have the living room set up. I thought I'd come see if you need help in the kitchen."

Callie let out a slow breath. "I don't know what to do with all of these boxes."

"Put them in the storage shed in the backyard. These little old cottages don't have basements or attics. That's why they put the shed in back."

Callie wrinkled her nose. "It smells like gasoline in there."

"It's only for a few months, right? Once you open your boutique, you can move someplace else if you want." Amanda waved her off. "I'm going to make you some food, and then we'll get your kitchen set up."

"Thank you," Callie sighed. She started for the aqua-tiled bathroom. Mom had made breakfast for her every day through high school but complained about it every morning.

Callie bit her bottom lip. Her chest hurt a little every time she thought of her mother. She'd never been good enough, smart enough or even ladylike enough for her mother. If it weren't for Amanda and her father, Callie wouldn't feel like she had any family at all. Now more than ever, she felt like she had their support.

She trotted into the kitchen after getting dressed and inhaled the smell of bacon and eggs.

"Bacon? Really?"

"I brought groceries," Amanda said in a sing-song voice.

"Thanks." Callie dropped into one of the four chairs around her refurbished oak dinette. "I appreciate it. Between checking out local places for staging pieces and getting started at the office, I've been crazy busy."

"Well, there's eggs, grits and toast, too." Amanda carried two plates over to the table and sat down. "We missed you at church this morning."

Callie shoveled a pile of eggs into her mouth. She hadn't been to church in years. Her prayers hadn't been answered when she needed help before, and skepticism had gotten the best of her. She mulled over going back to her family congregation after so long. Would it make any difference in her life?

"I'll go next week," she muttered.

Amanda's lips twitched at the corner. She picked up her fork. "So, what do you think of Ragland now? Are you glad to be back, Mark Chatham notwithstanding?"

Callie shrugged and said through a mouthful of food, "It has its charm, if you're into that."

Amanda laughed. "That's what you always say." She took a small bite of her bacon. "You always liked coming home for visits. It's not too different from Nashville, just smaller."

"No," Callie said. "It's nothing like living in the city."

Her sister smiled faintly. "You don't miss Ragland?"

"A little. I miss hanging out with friends, canoeing, the bonfires...you." *Mark.*

"We still have a lake here, you know. You can always canoe and have bonfires."

"It's not the same," argued Callie. "I'm older. I also need access to real shopping."

Amanda rolled her eyes. "It's not *that* bad here. I like shopping, too, I just don't have time to do much of it anymore." She looked up with a grin. "You don't know how it is with kids. They suck the life out of you. I love them more than anything, but all I do is clean house, fold laundry and play chauffeur."

"I don't know how Mom did it," Callie admitted. "I drove her nuts, but I guess I do miss her sometimes. Her chicken pot pie anyway."

"She didn't mean to be so hard on you. She just had dreams, and we were a part of them. I get it now with Justin and Nic. I want certain things for them, too. I want them to do things and like things that I do but..." Amanda flicked her thumb "...they have minds of their own."

"That's my problem," she joked. "I'm a terrible homemaker, and I have a mind of my own."

"That you do, little sis, but hey, kids love you."

Callie smiled because it was true. "So how often do Todd and Goldie hang out these days?" As Callie washed the breakfast dishes, her mind drifted back to yesterday and the rather enjoyable softball game.

"Goldie?" Amanda took a plate from her and dried it with a red-striped dish towel. "You mean Mark. Just every now and then. Mostly softball, I suppose."

"So they weren't playing softball when he first moved back?"

"You'd have to ask Todd. It's been a while now." Amanda walked over to a cabinet and opened it. "He came back around the time his mom was dying and then he stayed."

"His daughter was with him."

Amanda looked sideways at Callie. "Yes, she was a baby. I don't remember seeing them much."

"I remember you telling me the girl he married passed away or something."

"That's what I heard then, but I don't know the details. He's never mentioned it." She shrugged. "What does it matter?"

"He always seemed the small-town type until

he decided to join the Coast Guard. I was surprised he left."

Amanda put the plate away. "I guess so."

"It's just weird for me. First he leaves Ragland for the Coast Guard, and now he's a single dad running the Antique Market. He's changed."

"We all grow up some time."

"I guess." Callie picked up a fork to wash. "Maybe I have, too. I like to think so."

"You have, and remember, he was under a lot of pressure back then. He had a girlfriend everybody loved, baseball scouts coming around and he was only in high school."

Callie looked out of the window over the sink. "He joined the Coast Guard and ran off to the beach instead of accepting the offer to play for that Nashville minor league, dumping me along the way. The whole town was pretty put out, not just me. They figured he'd put Ragland on the map."

"Yes, but he's still sweet, just quiet and… I think unassuming is the word. I guess the minor leagues wasn't what he wanted."

"And neither was I."

Amanda nudged Callie with her elbow. "Maybe the timing just wasn't right. You ought to come to Todd's softball practices. Lots of cute guys hang around."

"No," Callie shot back. "Mark would be there, too. I much prefer a city boy, thank you."

Amanda laughed. "Yeah right, city mouse."

"There's nothing wrong with city life. I was very happy there—most of the time."

"I know you think so," Amanda relented. "I just don't believe it's you. I've seen you on the lake, and you like your blue jeans better than high heels."

Callie shrugged. "Why can't I have them both?"

Monday morning Jake Barton arrived early. Mark let the plumber in and showed him the disaster in the corner of the store. "I came in Saturday, and water was streaming from the joint in the ceiling, so I turned off all the water, and it's been drying out ever since."

The heavyset man with the dark goatee looked up. "Yeah, I see that," Jake drawled. He put his hands on his hips. The ceiling tile had been removed, and Lois had helped Mark pick up all the wet, mushy pieces. "Did you tape it up?"

"Best I could do. I could climb up there and do it myself, but I want to make sure it gets done right and that I don't miss anything."

"Yeah, I can fix that. Easy," Jake said. His

pale face flushed, and Mark thought he looked pleased.

"I'm going to try to run this through insurance," Mark said, "but I'm not sure if they'll take care of it. And I doubt the bank will cover this, even though they're technically the landlord."

"Good thinking." Jake ran his fingers across his stubbly chin. "What's upstairs?"

"It's just storage space, but there's a small bathroom from when someone lived up there a while back."

"Mind if I have a look?"

"No, of course." Mark motioned toward the back of the store.

Jake called over his shoulder, "Don't worry. I'll get her taken care of."

"Good. Thanks." Mark ambled back to the front counter just as the avocado-green phone on it rang. He hoped it was business and not the bank.

"Antique Market."

"Mark?"

"Yes."

There was a pause on the other end of the phone and then a woman took a breath. "This is Callie Hargrove."

Her face flashed in his mind and something inside of him clicked. "Yes?"

He couldn't believe she would pester him about the spoons again. At the same time, he felt strangely happy to hear from her. Mark leaned over the counter on one elbow. "They're still not for sale."

"I'm not calling about the spoons," she replied in an impatient voice.

He felt his grin widen. He couldn't help himself. "Then what can I do for you, Callie Hargrove?"

"Martin Realty has a farmhouse down near Bucksnort…" she stopped and giggled at the name of the road "…and it's been flipped."

"Are you selling it?" Mark asked.

"My sister's getting ready to as the agent. I'm staging. It's empty, and I need to pick up a hutch or a tall buffet. Just a few fillers."

"Okay." Hope burned in his chest. He could use a few big sales, and he sure didn't mind seeing her again. "Why don't you come down after lunch?"

"Great." She sounded cheery. "Do you have a delivery service? If not I can use Todd's truck."

"I do."

"I just have a little SUV. I mean, it works for some things but…"

"Delivery is no problem," Mark said.

"That'd be super. I'll see you after lunch then," Callie said. She sounded a bit breathless, like she meant it as a question. "And hey, about the spoons—"

"They're still not for sale, but I'll be here." A thump overhead jerked his attention up to the ceiling. It sounded like Jake was tearing the bathroom apart. "I need to go."

"Okay. See you in a bit." To his relief, she hung up with no awkward pause.

Why would it be awkward? he asked himself as he headed upstairs. She was just an old friend. Todd's sister-in-law.

The only regret he had from high school.

The bell over the door jingled and Callie looked around the Antique Market for Mark. She hadn't purposely decided to come to the shop again, but she needed the inventory. Determined to keep it professional, she took a deep breath and started working her way through the aisles, trying but failing to look over her shoulder at the spoon set.

She eyed the lovely spoons dangling like forbidden fruit on the wall, then turned her attention to the front corner by the window.

A bookcase filled with hardbacks stood on one side and pieces of mismatched china were on a stand beside it. She walked over and checked out the teacups and saucers on display. Some were chipped, while others looked in good condition. They were English except for the Blue Ridge plates from Appalachia. She picked one up and studied the hand-painted blossoms. Beautiful. She bent over and picked up a doll.

"Hello?"

Her heart trembled when she recognized his voice, but she ignored it and turned around and held out the doll. "Why do you have this thrown in an old cardboard box?"

Mark raised a brow. "It's a doll."

"Yes, but it's a collectible. This looks really old, and there's no wear and tear."

"I know." He walked over, calm and unruffled in his khakis and blue denim work shirt. "I don't really do toys, but my daughter likes to play with them. Someone donated it for free."

Callie struggled to keep her face impassive as a thousand questions about his daughter swirled in her mind. "Some of them are worth a lot. Have you checked the books or auction sites to see how much it's worth?"

He shook his head. "Not really. I have furniture to move. That value I know."

Callie motioned toward the shelves and dishes. "Your Blue Ridge china is underpriced, and you should value them at the going market rate and display them better."

"Lois handles most of those items."

"Oh." Callie smiled and wondered if Lois was a hundred years old. "I didn't mean to tell you how to run your business. I just hate to see things undervalued."

"I'll check into it. Thanks."

She held out the doll, and he stared for a second, then took it from her and carried it back to the counter. Unable to help herself, Callie added, "If your daughter really treasures it, maybe you should put it away for her."

Mark set down the toy. "What do you think of her?"

His question caught her off guard. "Of your daughter?"

"I mean," he probed, "you didn't seem surprised. By her existence."

She gave a sharp nod. She was here for furniture, not to dredge up painful memories.

He waited for her to speak.

Callie cleared her throat. She found the shining spoons soothing to look at instead of Mark's familiar blue gaze. "I heard about her when you moved back home. I think she was a baby then."

"It must have surprised you."

She smiled faintly. "No, not that you had a family. I mean, it happens eventually."

"Yes," he agreed, "I guess." He shifted his gaze away like he didn't want to look her in the face. "It happened fast. I mean…it was an impulsive relationship, and we eloped, and then it didn't work out, but by then Hadley was already on the way."

Callie studied him. His cheeks looked flushed. "I'm sorry," she said automatically. It was all she could think to say, but she meant it.

Mark straightened and glanced toward the back of the store.

Her eyes scanned the room for the pieces that had caught her eye last week. There was a hole in the ceiling in the back corner, and she saw an industrial fan. "You have a leak."

"Yes, last weekend."

Callie scrunched her brows. "Oh, what a mess." She realized the hutch was gone. "There was a tall walnut hutch back there last week. Circa 1940s."

"It has some water damage on top."

"Oh, I could fix it." Callie felt a surge of excitement. Maybe she could get a discount and turn it into something beautiful.

"Do you want to see it?"

She nodded.

Mark walked her to the back of the store. Footsteps echoed overhead. "Do you have a ghost?" she asked.

"My plumber's upstairs."

"Oh."

Mark walked over to a tarp and gave it a tug.

The hutch was pushed up against the wall, and stacks of cardboard boxes rested on either side of it like sentinels. It gleamed in the gloom of the overhead dim light bulb.

"You covered it up wet? It'll mildew." Callie put her hands on her hips and looked it over.

"No, it won't. I let it dry and ran a dehumidifier back here. See?" He motioned toward a small unit plugged in outside his office door.

"Yeah, but…" Callie shrugged. She crouched down and opened the lower cabinet doors. A whiff of musty air mixed with furniture polish hit her nose. The shelves were sturdy. "It's in good condition."

"I was asking four hundred, but I'd take three."

"Three? Really?" Callie frowned. It wasn't too bad a price. "With the water damage and the work I'm going to have to do on it, I think two fifty would be fairer."

"What work? It just needs a little touch-up on the top. You can't even see it."

"It didn't run down the back?" Callie tried to peer behind it.

"Well, yes, a little I suppose. How about two seventy-five?"

Callie calculated the budget that the realty office had issued her. It wasn't her money, but overspending was one of the reasons she had some debt. She was learning to curb her impulsiveness, though. "Fine." She ran her hand along the top shelves.

"What are you going to do with it anyway?" Mark folded his arms and watched her.

She took out her phone and pulled up pictures of projects that she kept in a folder marked Samples. Choosing the last hall table she'd magically brought from the 1960s into the new millennium, she held out her phone.

His eyes widened. "Blue?"

"It's chalk paint using an ombré technique." She pointed at the furniture legs. "See how it fades from blue into white and rust, then back down to the original stain at the feet?"

He looked horrified. "It looks psychedelic."

Callie dropped the phone back in her purse with a small huff. "The table's colorful and rustic, and for your information, everyone prefers blues and greens right now. Shabby chic on steroids."

His eyes shaded with doubt. "I've seen it in fancy boutiques and craft stores, but I didn't know it was that popular."

"You're old school." Callie smiled. "Nothing wrong with that. To be honest, some pieces I don't change. They're too beautiful, too regal. Some things just need to be cleaned up and left alone."

Mark nodded. "That's how I feel."

Callie looked back at the hutch. "This old hutch needs a new life, though. I'm thinking…" She backed away and studied it. "White. It suits a farmhouse. We'll do white and add some black or bronzed iron fittings."

Mark didn't seem as outraged at the idea of white paint. He studied the hutch, then shifted his gaze back to her. He seemed to be thinking something entirely different behind his eyes when he muttered, "White would be nice. I'm sure you'll do right by it."

She chuckled. "Can I look around some more?"

"Sure thing." He stepped back and let her pass. She led the way, feeling self-conscious. She was suddenly worried about how she looked.

She tried not to walk too fast to the front of the store. Mark returned to the register. Curious to explore, she rummaged through wooden bread boxes, paper towel holders and weird-looking farm implements until she found a brass basket.

It looked like a giant potato chip with a handle. She held it up. Mark was at the counter flipping through a book that held baseball cards.

"For carrying logs, right?"

He glanced up and nodded. "It's mostly for show, but sturdy enough to carry wood."

"I've seen these. They're cool." Callie lowered the basket and let it swing in her hand to feel the weight. "What era?"

He was still watching her when she looked up. "Uh…that one's about 1970s, but they've been around forever."

She met his gaze. "I'll take it."

"Great."

Callie headed to the front of the store and saw a tall square table handcrafted with narrow legs. Midcentury. Perfect. She'd take that, too.

"Do you still like baseball cards?" she called over her shoulder.

"I do, yes, but I'm going to sell these."

"That's too bad."

"Business is slow this year."

"Well, I'm glad you're still playing then."

There was such a long silence, she looked toward the counter. Mark redirected his attention to her from his book. "It's just softball these days."

"It's something, though, right? I was never good in sports, remember?"

"Yes, but you tried."

Callie picked up a silver candlestick holder that needed polishing. "I can't even walk straight half the time."

He laughed out loud, the first time she'd heard it since she'd been back, and it sounded deep and sweet, resurrecting memories—and feelings—she'd thought she'd erased forever.

"Sports aren't for everyone." Mark closed the book and crossed the room while she studied dozens of candlestick holders all over the place. "As long as you get some exercise, it's nothing to worry about."

"I still love canoeing," she blurted, then cringed. Where had that come from?

"Really? Yeah, that was kind of our thing, wasn't it?"

She tried to pretend he hadn't said it. "Actually, I like kayaking, too. I did a lot of it up in Tennessee."

"Those are sports, and you were always good at them."

She smiled. "I guess." He stood close, and it made her feel an awareness that she liked as much as she had at sixteen. Forcing her brain to focus, she pointed at the small table behind him. "I'll take the table, too. Fifty bucks?"

"It's marked seventy-five." He clearly didn't need to see the price tag.

"I'm not sure it's worth that but—"

"It's worth it." He slanted his head as if trying to figure her out.

She held up her hands in surrender. "I have to try. It's part of the job."

He chuckled. "I'll throw in a few candlestick holders."

"You do that." They held each other's eyes for a second, and Callie realized her heart was beating so loud in her ears that it drowned out the fan. "Okay, I'll take the hutch, the log carrier and the table for today, and I'm going to buy a half dozen of your candlestick holders."

He looked pleased but still said, "For one house?"

She shrugged. "I'll figure something out."

Grinning, Mark led her back to the counter and rang up her purchases.

"By the way," Callie said, remembering the vacant shop nearby, "do you know what the plans are for that storefront on the corner?"

He looked up. "No, not really. There used to be a dry cleaner's there." He held out the receipt.

Callie stuffed it into her back pocket and held out her hand. "I was just curious. I'm looking for a place to open a boutique."

"Is that so?"

"If I can manage it. Good doing business with you."

He eyed her hand for a moment like he didn't think she was serious, as if no one was ever friendly with him anymore, but he reached out and gave it a small shake. "Pleasure."

His hand felt warm and safe and wonderful. She wanted to hold it forever. With a start, she pulled away and looked out the window like she needed to check on her car.

"I'll deliver the hutch after I lock up here," he said. "The train depot, right?"

Collecting herself, Callie nodded. There were no words in her brain at the moment.

He waited for her response.

"There's a storage room around back on the track side. I'll meet you back there," she stammered.

"Okay. See you after five."

"Good deal." All of a sudden a tsunami of affection washed over her. She darted out the front door before he could tell.

Callie tossed the bag full of candlestick holders into the back seat and pulled out of the parking lot. What did it matter if Mark could see she was attracted to him?

She pulled up outside her office window. Studying the train depot, she realized she should be grateful she had a job staging furniture for the summer, even if she had to see Mark.

Maybe she really could make it here. Things seemed to be falling into place. She'd even survived seeing Mark again. She sucked in a long breath and let it out in a slow stream. Once upon a time, he'd swept her off her feet and then broken her heart, but that was eons ago. She was over it.

Mark caught himself smiling after Callie left the shop. She was still the same energetic, on-the-go girl, dashing out as quickly as she'd dashed in.

Traffic had eased. At lunchtime, the town square became congested with minivans and pickup trucks. He glanced through the window and saw the clock on the courthouse tower read one thirty.

Jake's footsteps came pounding down the stairs, so Mark walked back to meet him.

"It's a good thing you had the water turned off upstairs," Jake said.

"What's the problem?"

Jake held up a familiar-looking doll with a fish tail. "I'm pretty sure this mermaid stuck in a pipe was the root of your problem."

He grinned, and Mark tried to keep from groaning. Most people in town had seen Hadley in action, either at the market or the ball field or the grocery store. "How much do I owe you for today?"

"I can fix the leak, change out the damaged

flooring up there, and put another ceiling tile in for you for about five hundred dollars."

Mark nodded. His gut instincts told him insurance wouldn't cover a pipe clogged by a preschooler's doll. He would have to sell his baseball card collection for sure, and that meant money not going to the bank for the late rent. "Sounds fair," he agreed, "although I can replace the ceiling tile myself."

Jake trotted out to his truck with a promise to return later that day.

Mark soon realized he was starved. He generally ate his lunch late after the lunch crowd and shoppers had dwindled down. Grabbing his ball cap and sunglasses from behind the counter, he strode to the door and flipped the sign from Open to Closed and headed to the Grub 'n' Go.

The front windows were painted with giant red block letters, and there were farm animals holding forks and knives drawn on the walls. He'd eaten there all of his life.

He pulled opened the bright red door and walked in, his shoulders relaxing at the comforting smells of grilled hot dogs and deep-fried onion rings. A chalkboard on the wall announced that Tuesday's specials were the bacon avocado BLT, the Italian sub and the mushroom burger.

The cashier, Gabby Hayes, fresh out of high

school, smiled at him. "Hi, Mr. Chatham, what'll you have today?"

He wondered if he came in too often. "Mushroom burger, onion rings and a Coke, please."

Her wavy hair reminded him of Callie in high school.

"Will that be all?" she asked.

"Yes, thanks, that's it."

"How's Hadley doing?"

"She's good. She's in pre-K these days."

"For the summer?"

"It's a special program."

She nodded like she understood, and Mark handed her cash, picked up a number in a metal stand to set on his table and went to fill his cup at the soda fountain. He tried not to feel ancient. With a forlorn thought, he realized forty wasn't *that* far away anymore, and he was still alone.

He corrected himself. He wasn't alone. He had a wonderful daughter. Hadley was his life now.

The corner table by the front window was free, and Mark walked over, sipping his soda. Folks outside ambled up and down the sidewalks, hurrying from the law office, the drugstore or the courthouse. He sat down to people-watch.

"Goldie?"

He looked up with a start. Darla Perez stood

beside him, holding a giant fruit smoothie. "How are you, Darla?" Remembering his manners, Mark stood up to shake her hand.

"I'm doing fine. I haven't seen you since the summer preschool orientation. How are you and Hadley doing? Is she liking school?"

He glanced out the window, certain he shouldn't tell the mother of his daughter's classmate that Hadley hated it and threw a fit every morning when they had to leave. "She's doing okay, I suppose, although she'd prefer to go to work with me."

Darla gave him a sympathetic smile. "I know it's hard, believe me. It doesn't seem like a bad idea for her to hang out with you at work," she added. "I thought it was cute seeing her running around the Market."

Mark appreciated her kindness. Hadley often wreaked havoc on the days he brought her to the Market with him. "The doctor thought it'd be a good idea to have her play with other children before she started kindergarten."

Darla nodded. "I know it's been a rough start, but I haven't heard anything much since she cut Logan's hair with the teacher's scissors."

"I'm so sorry about that."

"Oh, it's okay." Darla waved him off. "I'm sure my son was just as involved."

Mark grimaced. "She spends a lot of time

in time-out." He didn't mention the constant stream of notes reporting his daughter pushing and hitting other children.

Darla patted him on the arm. "Hang in there. If I can survive three boys, you can handle a sweet busy bee like Hadley."

"Thanks," he murmured.

"It's no problem," she reassured him. "Let Calvin and I know if there's anything we can do for you."

Mark nodded, somewhat embarrassed that half the town knew he needed parenting advice. She hurried off as her cell phone rang, and he sat back down.

At that moment, Gabby brought his food over. For a moment, he felt guilty as he sank his teeth into the burger. He'd packed Hadley a half sandwich, clumsily chopped carrot sticks and two graham crackers. Lois did better, and thinking of Callie's attention to detail, he imagined she would be a marvel. He wondered what she'd think of his little girl and what she thought of him as a father.

He closed his eyes and made a promise to himself to take Hadley out for a treat on the weekend.

Chapter Four

Callie found herself at a real estate listing at four thirty. She would miss the delivery from the Antique Market. She frowned at every forgotten cobweb in the corners of the Pierce farmhouse. The cleaning crew had done a pretty good job, but Callie couldn't work her magic with spiderwebs fluttering in the drafts.

She glanced around the room and imagined which pieces would work best where. Admiring the original wood floors, she trotted to the kitchen to decide on a position for the hutch. Mark had said he'd deliver everything to the depot around five. She glanced at the time on her phone again. She still had the bedrooms upstairs to reevaluate, and that meant she'd end up trying new layouts until she was exhausted. She hated to miss him, although she wondered if seeing him so often was a good idea. It seemed every time she did, she spent the rest of the day convincing herself the past was the past.

She noticed she'd missed a call from Amanda and hit the call back button.

"Hey!" Her sister sounded out of breath. "Are you still at the farmhouse?"

Callie nodded despite being on the phone. "Yes. This place is stunning, but your crew missed some cobwebs on the ceiling."

"Oh, no. I'll send someone back out. How long are you going to be?"

"I wanted to look over the bedrooms again, but I'll probably head back soon."

"You might as well. They took out every light bulb they could get their fingers on before the place was auctioned off. You won't have any light."

"Yes, I noticed that," Callie complained. She started up the back stairs that led to a bedroom in a narrow tower. "The tiles have to stay, of course, unless you want to flip the whole bathroom, but I like the black-and-white tile. It's retro."

"I think so, too."

"The place is gorgeous. Practically a Victorian," Callie said. She looked down the gorgeous upstairs hall of the house where the original trim still framed the doorways. "They don't make them like this anymore."

Her sister made a sound of agreement.

"By the way," Callie added, "I saw Mark again today. I bought a few things from his shop, so I have a hutch coming in this afternoon that needs to be put in the storage room."

"Who's bringing it over?"

"He is."

"I didn't know he made deliveries."

"I didn't want to bother Todd, and Mark said he had a truck anyway."

"That was nice of him." Callie could hear her sister smiling through the other end of the phone. "Don't you think he's still a good-looking guy?"

"It doesn't matter. It's just business." Callie rolled her eyes at her sister through the phone as she walked into the master bedroom. There was nothing but an old dresser against the wall. "This dresser's a piece of junk," she mumbled.

"That's why they left it. Might as well work your magic on it. We don't have to sell it with the house, we just need it to look good."

"All right." Callie sighed. "I've already reserved those twin beds in storage. We'll need them here. We have to find some kind of showpiece for this master bedroom."

Amanda groaned. "We don't have the budget for something like that."

Callie's heart sank with frustration. "I'll figure something out."

"Great. How about dinner? What time do you think you'll be back?"

Callie glanced through a bare window at the heavy beams of afternoon sunshine. "Maybe six?"

"That'll work. Come on over as soon as you're done."

"Your house?"

Amanda laughed. "Of course my house. I've got two kids and the old ball and chain. It's spaghetti night."

"Nice. I'll be there."

Spaghetti with the family sounded wonderful to Callie, and besides, she loved seeing the kids more often now.

The driveway at Amanda's house had no room for Callie, with the minivan and Todd's truck taking up space. He high-fived her when he answered the door and told her she didn't have to knock. "Amanda's in the kitchen," he said, walking back to the couch.

Callie raised a brow at him as she passed through the living room. "Why aren't you helping her?"

He waved the television remote. "She said I could watch baseball."

The kitchen smelled like garlic and bread.

"I've died and gone to heaven." Callie slumped down onto the wooden bench at the dinner table. Amanda had her back to her, doing a hundred things at once.

"Do you want me to help? You look like an octopus."

Her sister laughed. "No, I got it. You know I like to do it myself. But you can set the table."

Callie obeyed, getting up to explore the cupboards.

"Did you get finished up at the farmhouse?" Amanda asked.

Callie nodded. "I have some notes and sketches. I'll finalize the layout soon. All I need to do now is find a bed frame, get a hold of that hutch and get it stripped down."

Amanda put down a spoon with a clatter and licked her finger. "That'll be cute. Are you sure you don't want to repaint the walls?"

Callie's stomach rumbled. She found the plates and grabbed a stack of five. "I'd repaint it if it was mine, but the white works. I wouldn't waste the money."

"You waste money?" Amanda looked at her and laughed.

"I know, I know," Callie said in mock defense. "I'm trying to do better."

"Well, if you've almost paid off your credit

cards, you can start saving for a lease on a shop. Just stay focused."

"I'm trying." Callie rifled through the kitchen drawers for silverware. "Where'd you get this?" She held up a spoon.

"They're new."

"They're cute. I really like them." Callie held up a butter knife and studied the handle. "I liked your old ones, though."

"It doesn't matter," Amanda pouted. "They're pretty and shiny and I like them."

"Speaking of pretty and shiny," Callie said, "Mark thinks that every time I walk into that shop I'm there to bother him about the spoons. Thing is, he's right. They're gorgeous. I can't figure out why he won't let them go other than they belonged to his mother and grandmother."

Amanda turned off the stove burners, then collapsed onto the bench beside her. "He does okay business, but he definitely has a mind of his own. I tried to help him move the hutch in when he came by the depot this afternoon, but he flat out refused."

Callie wrinkled a brow. "He moved that thing all by himself?"

"No, he had help. Jake Barton was there, and Hadley came along, so I was running back and forth trying to keep her off the train tracks. I thought Mark would lose his mind."

Callie could imagine him chiding his daughter over and over. She was liking this little girl more and more. "Did they get it moved in okay?"

"Yeah, that and another table."

"The tall side table?" Callie asked. "He gave me a good deal on the hutch, so I bought the table, too."

Amanda grinned. "I'm sure he did."

"It was just business."

"Well, he's still totally single. I can't remember the last person he dated."

The brief haunted look she'd caught in Mark's eyes when he mentioned his elopement stabbed Callie with guilt. "Do you think it's anything I did? Is there something wrong with me?" Her eyes bloomed with tears against her will.

"There's nothing wrong with you." Amanda leaned over and gave her a long hug. "Just live your life until the man you're meant to grow old with shows up at your door."

Callie sighed. "I already am old."

Amanda laughed. "You're not even in your prime. Don't worry about it. Live your life until you meet someone you don't want to let go of, then settle down."

"I tried that once."

The sound of the kids running around the backyard broke up the quiet. Callie felt the corners of her mouth twitch. "I guess it worked out, though, because I didn't end up with a house full of rug rats."

Amanda stood up. "You'll want rug rats one of these days."

Callie smiled. "Maybe."

Chapter Five

Mark slept like the dead the Tuesday night after a two-hour practice at the softball field. Luckily, Lois had watched Hadley, but they both still went to bed late.

When he dragged himself into Hadley's room to wake her up the next morning, he found his daughter under the bed with her legs sticking out. Her wiggling feet told him she was awake. He slunk down onto the floor. She was still unaware of his presence. Her ankles bobbed up and down, and he grabbed one of her toes and tickled it.

She giggled. Then a thump from underneath the bed told him she'd bumped her head. He chuckled as the feet disappeared out of sight, then her bright eyes emerged out from under the rail.

"Daddy." Her irritated frown made him smile.

"Daddy, what?"

"I know that was you, Daddy."

He leaned down so their noses almost touched. "What are you doing under there?"

A sly looked passed over her face. "Nothing."

"Uh-huh."

Hadley pursed her lips, then stuck her arm out. She was holding his best flashlight.

"Give me that," he chided, taking it from her as she wormed her way out from beneath the bed. Her rumpled blue-and-white nightgown had a dusty streak over the chest. She sat up and stared at him adorably.

"What were you doing with Daddy's flashlight?"

Hadley sniffed, wiped her nose with the back of her hand and sat down beside him. She had a red crayon in her other hand.

Mark closed his eyes and counted to five. "Were you coloring under the bed?"

"No. Can I go to work with you today?"

"No."

She frowned, and her shoulders slumped.

"Hadley, what were you doing with the crayon under the bed?"

She wiggled her feet back and forth, pretending like she didn't hear him.

"What did you do?" Mark hated to sound

angry, but he didn't have time to clean up another mess.

"I don't know."

"Yes, you do."

"I don't want to go to school."

Mark scooped her up.

She melted into him. "Can I go to the Market with you?"

He wrapped his arms around her and dropped his head back onto the bed behind him. "Again, no, but you can stay with me after school."

"I don't like Lois's house, it smells like—" She pinched her nose and shook her head.

Mark chuckled and squeezed her. "Well, that's just cabbage you smell. They eat a lot of it."

Hadley held on to her nose. "I don't like it."

Mark took the crayon out of her other fist and set it on her antique nightstand. It'd been his mother's table. "Did you color on the floor under the bed?"

"No." She buried her face in his armpit. "The air box is ugly."

"The what? Do you mean the vent?" Mark sighed. "You colored the air vent?"

"It's not dirty anymore."

"Thank you," he said in a wry tone. "Did you color on the floor?"

"No."

"Good. Now we need to get ready for work."

"I'm going with you?"

"No, my work is the Market. Yours is school."

"I hate school."

"It's not so bad. You get to play outside and have treats. Let's get ready now."

"No."

Mark tried to sit her up, but she cowered in his lap.

"Come on, baby girl. Daddy can't be late." He could almost hear the wheels turning in her head, looking for excuses. He stood up, then set her on the bed. "What do you want to wear today?"

"I didn't say my prayers."

"You said them last night."

"I need to say them again because I forgot something."

He exhaled to keep from losing his patience. "Okay. Let's do it." He knelt down the way Lois had taught her to do, and she jumped up beside him and steepled her little palms.

With eyes wide open, she said, "Dear God, bless me so I won't have to go to school today. Bless my hair, and bless Daddy...and I want a mommy and a cat." She stopped and looked up at him with a twinkle in her eye.

"I told you maybe Santa will bring you a kitten," he stuttered, trying to sound stern. Her prayer for a mommy was a new addition. His mind swirled over the fact she'd tapped into his most nagging worry—that and the fact she'd mentioned her hair again. She hated having it combed.

"I want a dog for Christmas, too," Hadley added, scrambling up onto the bed.

"Maybe." Mark pointed toward her closet. "Go pick out your clothes and dress yourself like a big girl."

She frowned, and he waited for the usual explosion. "I'll let you do your own hair," he said, but to his surprise, she looked crestfallen. "Do you want me to brush it for you then?"

Hadley flopped back on the bed and crossed her arms stubbornly. "I hate hair. I hate my hair. I hate *all* hair," she announced.

Mark shook his head as he left the room, hoping she was dressed by the time he was ready to go.

He gave her a ball cap to wear in exchange for promising not to cry on the way to school. Her eyes welled up with tears, but he carried her inside and told the teacher she could wear the hat all day long if she liked. He hoped no one noticed her hair hadn't been brushed.

Mark had been in such a rush to open the shop on time, he was pretty sure he'd forgotten to lock the door to the garage. Leaning over the front counter, he picked up an old salt shaker someone had dropped off in a donation box. The salt-and-pepper set was a find. They were vintage Fire-King with Dutch tulips painted on each bottle. The phone rang, and he mumbled a greeting as he balanced it between his ear and shoulder.

"Mark? Hi, it's Callie."

He cleared his throat to collect himself and took a deep breath. "Yes, hi, Callie."

"Hey, I have a question for you." Her voice sounded tense.

"Is everything okay? Did you get the hutch the other night?"

"Yes, thank you, I got the hutch. By the way," she added, "I'm looking for a bed frame now. A big one, but not expensive. Something elegant for a master bedroom in a farmhouse that I wish I hadn't left today with my gas gauge on empty."

He repositioned the phone in his hand. "I'm sorry. What?"

She laughed at herself, but it was stiff.

"Are you okay?"

She sighed into the phone. "I'm on the highway that runs past the old mill. You know, the one that comes into town past the library?"

"Three seventy-one. What are you doing out there?"

"I ran out of gas."

He couldn't hold back a smile, but at least he didn't laugh out loud. "Again? I would have guessed you'd outgrown that habit."

"Yes," she answered, sounding anxious. "I know you've come to my rescue before, but that was then. Look, I just forget to watch for the fuel light to come on, and now I'm in the middle of nowhere with a hole in the wall, and I'm not going to make it to the hardware store and back before nightfall."

"How'd you get a hole in a wall?" Endearing as she was, Mark had no idea what she was talking about.

"Could you come get me? My sister's with a client, my brother-in-law and father aren't answering their phones, and I really don't have anyone else to call." She tried to cover her embarrassment with a chuckle, but it didn't work.

"It must be eighty-five degrees outside by now," he said to sympathize with her.

"Sure feels like it."

"Yep, I'm on my way." Mark realized he hadn't thought the scenario through as he said it. It was near lunchtime, business would pick up, and if the Market closed, he would miss the most lucrative part of his sales day. He grimaced until her sweet voice filled his ear.

"Thank you so much, Mark. I feel ridiculous, but your number was in my cell phone."

"It's not a problem," he told her. "Let me close up, and I'll be there in thirty minutes or so."

She breathed loudly with relief. "Thank you!"

"You get back in the car and stay out of the sun," he advised, "but leave the doors open."

"I will," she assured him. "I know the drill."

"And don't get into a car with any strangers," he added.

She laughed. "I've had three pass me so far, and no one stopped to help."

"They must not be from around here."

"You're right. No one from Ragland would do that."

He said goodbye and hung up. Before heading to the back room to find something to put gasoline in, he locked the front door. It was terrible timing, but what could he do? He couldn't just leave her out there to melt.

A half hour passed before he saw Callie standing outside her car. It wasn't unbearable heat, but it was still hot. He thought her hair looked damp around her temples and wondered why she didn't pull it up. He'd always loved her hair in a ponytail.

"Hi," she said, darting over to the driver's side of the truck before he could get out.

"Are you doing okay?" Her face was shiny with sweat.

She wiped her damp forehead and laughed at herself. "Yes, there's a cross breeze with both windows down. I just got out when I saw a car coming."

Mark leaned over the bed of the pickup and pulled out the gallon of gas.

Callie clapped her hands together. "Thank you so much. What do I owe you?"

"You don't owe me anything."

"Of course I do. You bought that and drove all the way out here. I know it's costing you money."

He smiled before heading to her car. "Haven't you ever had anyone do anything for you just to be nice?"

"Not without strings attached." She followed behind him, her shoes crunching on the roadside's pea-size gravel.

He started to chuckle but realized she was serious. "Maybe you ought to find better company," he chided.

Tall grass grew in tangled bunches on the side of the road, but she'd pulled over far enough to avoid any oncoming traffic. Smart girl. He unscrewed the cap.

"I can do that," she said. Gas gurgled as he poured the contents of the small container into the tank. The car guzzled every drop. The sun beat down on his shoulders, and Mark glanced back at Callie. "I know you can. How long have you been out here?"

Callie pulled her phone out of her pocket and checked the time. "Just about an hour or so. I'm fine." Her face looked flushed. Perspiration dotted her upper lip and her forehead.

"Looks like you're melting to me," he teased.

"I've handled worse. You of all people should know I can take care of myself. I just forgot to fill the tank yesterday and didn't see the low fuel light on until it was too late."

"Well," he said, as he tipped the jug for the remaining gas, "you may want to keep a small can of gas in the back from now on, just in case."

"I could have walked," Callie said, shrugging like it was only a block or two back into town. "It's just hot, and I have so much to do, and…"

"It's no problem, Callie. Besides, I'm sure you'd have done the same for me."

Her lips broke out into that charming smile. "Of course I would have."

"I believe you."

She held out some cash to him. "Here. Thanks for helping me out."

He ignored it, walked past her and tossed the empty container back over the tailgate.

"Take it," she said again louder, coming up behind him.

"Your money's no good here," he joked. When he turned around, she stood close and looked flustered.

"I need to pay you for the gas and your time. I bet you had to close the shop to do this."

Another streak of admiration shot through him. No one else would have thought about that. "I tell you what. I was going to head to the Grub 'n' Go to get some ice cream, maybe a burger. You go with me, and I'll let you buy."

Her face lit up. "I'm starving! We'll have to hurry, but I'd love to buy you lunch."

He quietly laughed. "Do you want to leave the car here and ride with me?"

She hesitated. "No," she said, swallowing, "I'll just follow you over." Her thick brows lowered over her golden eyes like she was trying to hide something.

Mark cleared his throat. "The Grub 'n' Go hasn't changed. Same old burgers and milkshakes."

"I know. I've already been in once since I've been back." She pretended to look sheepish.

"I know what you mean. I'm there every week." Callie chuckled as he added, "Follow me."

He headed for the truck parked behind her

car, but snuck a glance back at her retreating figure. Mark wondered if her mind was swimming with memories, too. She'd once followed him to baseball games, out to the lake and even to the Grub 'n' Go, but that was a long time ago. This was just business and a neighborly lunch. At least that's what he told himself.

Callie kept pace with Mark's truck, resisting the urge to speed up. He still drove like an old man, slow and steady. She could do better than forty-five on a country highway.

As they came into town, her mouth started to water. She pulled into the parking lot and parked beside Mark. As she skipped around her car to meet him, she teased, "The Grub 'n' Go is looking quaint these days."

He beamed. "Quaint enough you'll find yourself here more than you ever were." Inside, the familiar smell of burgers drifted through the air along with chatter. He motioned for her to go ahead, but she stayed beside him until they stood in line together.

Callie scanned the menu and decided on the bacon cheeseburger and a chocolate shake. "Hey." She nudged him. "How do you know I'm not into health food now?"

Mark snorted under his breath. "Because I don't think you're skin and bones."

"I'm not sure whether to be offended by that or not." Callie laughed. She definitely wasn't a beanpole, but she couldn't eat burgers and fries every day. "I do try to eat healthy," she clarified. "Salads, water, lots of protein."

He gave her a wink. "You don't have to convince me, and burgers are protein."

Callie took a deep breath, inhaling the scent of fried food with pleasure. "They certainly are."

They ordered, then found a table. For a split second, Callie's glance drifted to the back corner booth where she and Mark had spent many hours with their friends, but she shook it off as they sat by the front window. She accepted that he still wasn't much of a talker, so she got the ball rolling by talking about the farmhouse she'd just examined out in the country. He knew exactly where it was.

Their order came quickly, and Mark thanked Gabby, who grinned at them both as if she knew a secret. Callie ignored the subtle approval and pretended to concentrate on her plate. "Oh, my," she exclaimed through a mouthful of meat and lettuce, "this is still so wonderful."

As they ate, Callie told him about living in Nashville. He surprised her when he asked, "Did you accomplish what you set out to do?"

She furrowed her brow.

He shrugged. "Todd never says much."

"Oh." Callie wondered how much Todd talked about her to Mark. "Well, I wanted to be an interior designer, and I liked the country music scene. So I moved to Nashville and found an apartment to share. My roommate, Tracey, wanted to be a musician, so she hung out at the honky-tonks. Two other girls roomed with us. Four of us in that apartment was tight, but I lived there for about a year and a half until I had a good job. Then I found something downtown so I could be closer to work."

"Did you go to school or do any real estate up there?" He stuck a fry in his mouth and listened, with his steady gaze.

A flower of warmth bloomed in Callie's chest. It felt good to talk. Sometimes she could hardly get a word in edgewise with Amanda. She shook her head. "I worked for an upscale furniture store and took night classes for a two-year interior design program."

Mark looked mystified, so she added, "The store was very fancy. It's on Hillsboro Pike, you know?"

He shook his head.

"Kind of like Peachtree Street in Atlanta."

"Oh, yeah." He nodded.

"There were designers on staff, and I worked under them. The plan was to eventually open my own boutique." She paused, then took a deep breath. "Well, that hasn't worked out yet. That's why I'm home for the summer. Amanda convinced me to give it a go here."

Mark gave her a sympathetic smile. "I wish you luck then."

"Oh, don't worry. If it doesn't work, I still have contacts up there. In the meantime," she added with a sigh, "I'm working for Mr. Martin at the real estate office."

Mark took a sip of his soda. "So you're going to try to open your place here in Ragland first."

"Yes, if I can find an affordable spot. I'm checking out the empty store on the corner of the square." She shrugged. "If I can't make it work in a few months, there's always Nashville. In the meantime, I'll spend time with my sister and her kids."

"Family time is never wasted," Mark murmured.

When their eyes met, she wondered if he was thinking about his parents or the mother of his child. She cleared her throat. "So what about you? Have you been working at the Antique Market since you came back to Ragland?"

"Mostly." Mark hesitated, but Callie knew to wait patiently. "After I joined the Coast Guard out of high school, I was based down in Florida.

After five or six years there, I came back home because Mom was sick."

"Oh, I see."

Mark shifted his gaze out the window. "I had Hadley by then. She was a baby. I'd just gotten custody and had no idea what I was doing."

"That must have been hard."

He looked up suddenly. "My wife—her name was Lisa—we separated before Hadley was born, and then she died there. At the hospital, I mean."

"How awful."

Mark looked grim. "Yes. I was getting ready to reenlist, but I took Hadley and came home. Lisa's only family was her father—a commercial fisherman. He wasn't interested in getting to know his granddaughter."

Callie stared at her plate. It sounded like a heart-wrenching movie, not something that could ever happen to Ragland's golden boy. When she looked up at him, he was watching her.

"You were gone by then," he said. "My parents were older when I was born, remember? By the time I was in my early twenties, they had health problems. Mom passed soon after Dad, and it's just been me and Hadley the past few years."

Callie dipped her chin in sympathy. "Well, it looks like you're doing okay."

He didn't agree with her but mused, "I know you lost your mom, too."

"Our mom died from a stroke two years after I graduated." Callie's mood sank and began to drag like she was stuck in a marsh. She swallowed. "I felt awful because we weren't speaking to each other at the time. She was furious I'd moved so far away."

Mark didn't say anything. He just nodded and let Callie go on.

"We didn't get along much when I was a kid," she sighed. "I couldn't stay focused in school, and I was more interested in talking or playing outside than staring at books. My sister was the good daughter. I was always into trouble even before I could walk."

"That's not true," Mark replied.

Callie's eyes almost filled with tears. She lifted her shoulders in a helpless shrug. "I just didn't feel like Ragland was for me. I mean, you were gone, most of my friends had left and Mom and I couldn't get along. Then she was so mad when I left."

"Your parents were happy Amanda stayed here?"

"Yes, but she never wanted to live anywhere else. Besides, I think my parents thought Nashville was just full of wannabe singers and musicians."

"Is it?"

She grinned. "Kinda. I just wanted to find somewhere to make my mark, and I have. I can design, and I can make old things look new, like the farmhouse. Wait and see, my boutique will be full of beautiful, repurposed pieces."

"How's that house coming along?" Mark raised a brow. "It's the old Pierce house, right?"

"Yes, that's right. I don't remember it much." He didn't respond, and she realized she was talking about herself too much. "Have you ever thought about going back to Florida?"

Mark's eyes sparked. "I still love the coast," he admitted. "I think when I retire someday, I'll buy a vacation house around Jekyll Island and stay in state."

"That'd be awesome. Right on the water?"

He nodded. "That way I can fish from the shore and not have to take a boat out every day."

"You have a boat?"

"Not right now, no." Mark leaned forward. "But I know what I want. Something for fishing and high speed, but up here you don't need anything much better than a bass boat."

"Unless you like to water-ski," she pointed out.

"I thought you liked canoes?"

Callie melted a little at his reference to their past. "I do. I used to have a kayak, but I left it in Nashville."

"Oh, yeah? We still have a couple canoes in the barn."

"You do?" Callie reached for her milkshake, but her mind whirled with ways she could politely ask to borrow one.

"Sure. We never got rid of them."

"I remember you used to let the gang use them. I didn't realize you were still at your parents' house."

"Yes, down Barmill Road. I just have the house and a few acres left these days."

Callie started to lean forward but realized she'd be too close to him. She sat back. "You're really lucky," she said. "Dad still lives in the same old subdivision out there in the county."

"Well, no wonder you didn't love it here. Every girl needs a canoe."

"And an ATV."

He laughed. "I have a couple of those, too. I have a whole garage and outbuilding full of stuff."

"Sounds like you have some inventory you need to move," Callie joked. "I would outright buy a canoe from you."

"That so? Well, you should probably try one out first. What are you doing on Saturday?"

Callie blinked. Was he asking her on a date? "I—"

Mark shrugged. "If you want to borrow one, you're welcome to anytime."

"Okay," she replied, hoping he hadn't read her mind. "I may need a buddy, though, if I can't talk Amanda into it."

"Yeah? I'm free on Saturdays for the most part. Lois comes in to manage the shop."

"Lois, right," Callie said with a mischievous look. "I've been meaning to ask her about some spoons."

Mark jokingly narrowed his eyes. "The spoons will never be for sale. They're priceless."

"That's why I want them," she teased. "Why are they priceless? I don't remember ever seeing them at your house."

"They were put away. I dug them out after Mom died and made a display case for them."

"You did a great job. Where'd they come from?"

"My triple-great-grandmother was sent those spoons by the love of her life after the Civil War."

"For real?" Callie felt a renewed spike of interest. "I didn't know they were that old."

"Long story short," he said, "they were passed down to me as a reminder of loyalty and love."

"I'd love to hear the whole story someday."

Callie pulled her phone out and checked the time. "But it's getting late."

"I'll tell you the rest on Saturday on the canoe trip."

She got to her feet, and he stood to walk her out. "Tell me the end, at least," she said.

Mark's mouth twitched at the corner, although he kept his gaze straight ahead. Callie knew he was aware of looks from some of the patrons in the diner. People who knew him. People who remembered her. She ignored it as they walked out, and instead she admired how his hair curled at the ends around his ears like a little boy's. "Please?"

He reached out and touched her elbow, and for a second Callie thought he might hold her hand. "There were spoons, a wedding and then a family came along."

She smiled. Reaching her car, she dug into her pocket for her keys. "I better get back to that farmhouse and fix the mess I made. They have another house they want me to look at later."

Mark raised a hand in a wave and walked on to his pickup. "See you later, Callie."

The car was as hot as the surface of the sun when she climbed in. She turned it on and kicked up the air-conditioning, then noticed Mark had stopped. She rolled down the window and leaned out.

"Don't forget to get gas," he called.

She laughed and waved him off like he was silly. It was nice that he still knew her so well, even after all this time.

When Mark returned to the store, he found a message on the archaic answering machine in his office.

"Hi, Mark! This is Joy Cavanaugh."

He leaned forward in his seat. Joy was his biggest customer. She came in almost every month and bought several things to take up to the markets in Atlanta.

"I just wanted to let you know that I'm going to be moving in a few weeks. My mother's been sick, and she's up in North Carolina. I'm shutting the house up for now and wanted to let you know how much I appreciate your business. It really meant a lot, and I hope I'll see you when I get back." She ended with a phone number with a North Carolina area code.

Mark slumped in his seat, and the once pleasant taste of a burger on his tongue turned to bitterness. His swirling thoughts about Callie faded into the background.

Joy had sometimes bought antiques from him worth up to a thousand dollars. It was money he couldn't do without. He realized he wasn't breathing and took a gasping breath that reverberated in the silence of the store.

It was happening. He was going to lose the store, his parents' pride and joy and, besides his house, the only source for employment and retirement he had. Everyone would talk about how the Chathams ran that old shop for generations until their son came along and lost it to the bank. He'd be a disappointment. Again.

The phone jangled, and the shrill sound made him jump. He wasn't ready to speak to Joy, and he certainly didn't want to hear from the bank. It rang insistently, and he finally picked it up with a frown.

"Antique Market."

"Mr. Chatham?"

The voice sounded familiar. "Yes?" Mark wrinkled his forehead.

"This is Mrs. Pennington from Little Steps Academy. I'm afraid we have a problem this afternoon."

Mark's heart sank. "Oh, no. Is Hadley okay?"

"Well," the school's principal continued, "she's in my office screaming at the top of her lungs because she refuses to sit in the time-out chair, and I have another parent on the way."

Mark closed his eyes. His first instinct was to say, *What has she done now?* but instead he said calmly, "I'm on my way." He hung up and rubbed his forehead. Closing up again to pick up Hadley was another hour of sales lost, and he'd just returned from lunch. He sighed tiredly.

The lights were just coming on over the softball fields. Crowds of children ran around barefoot, and mothers and fathers shouted at their Little League players to quit chasing butterflies.

Pushing the bad week with Hadley to the back of his mind, Mark climbed out of the truck and grabbed his equipment bag. He needed to hit some balls. A swing and crack of the bat would release the negative energy that had seeped into his bones.

"Goldie! How are you?"

The familiar voice ruined Mark's newfound contentment on the way to the Copperheads' practice field.

A trim, athletic form jogged up beside him. Matt McIntyre, his banker, had been muscular in high school and tried to keep in shape. He probably had a gym membership. He could afford it.

"Hey, are you playing tonight?" McIntyre asked.

Mark kept on walking. "Practice," he replied.

"Oh," the man said in a casual tone. "We have a game on field six."

Mark didn't reply, hoping he'd go away without bringing anything up.

"So," fished McIntyre. "Have you thought about selling any more land?"

"I already did, McIntyre. I'm not selling any more."

The man acted incredulous. "What's a few more acres?"

Mark sighed to keep from losing it. "I don't want to sell any more land."

The banker persisted. "You have, what? Nine or ten acres left? You could sell off what's across the road."

Mark glanced at him, then over at his team's field. He knew the banker was aware there were only eight acres left. The house was down to five on one side, but thankfully the people who'd bought the land behind him hadn't messed with it. It was still just grown-over fields that once produced cotton, peanuts and tobacco.

"There is the rent, you know," McIntyre reminded him. They came to a stop, with the Copperheads' practice one way and McIntyre's game the other.

Mark forced himself to look McIntyre in the eye. "I'm almost caught up for May on the shop. I'll get that in, and I'll have June's by July."

"And July?"

That left him speechless. The ball fields

weren't the place to talk about overdue payments. Mark realized his mouth hung open. He snapped it shut and said in a hard voice, "I will be completely caught up by August."

McIntyre nodded. "Okay. But just so you know, we made a nice profit on your last parcel of land and would be happy to take some more off your hands."

Mark gave McIntyre a sharp nod. "Thanks for letting me know. Have a nice game."

He walked off before anything else was said. Of course, he was lucky they'd given him the option to trade a few acres in to cover his debts, but McIntyre was greedy. He'd started snatching up acreage like a hoarder when the population began to grow.

Not Mark's land. He was keeping his land around the house *and* the field across the street—for Hadley. Not that she deserved it at the moment. She'd pulled the hair of one of the little girls at school.

His chest pinched at the thought that selling off all the land would settle his overdue rent and a lot of other problems, but he had to honor his family. He'd sold the baseball card collection, but it still wasn't near enough. He was running out of options and really only had the spoons left. But those were too special.

The thought ran through his mind that going

back to Florida to start over was an option. But then he shook his head as he strode toward the dugout.

He belonged to Ragland, and Ragland belonged to him. He wasn't leaving.

Chapter Six

Callie drove out to the Pierce farmhouse, her mind mulling over the week. She was grateful Mark had been available to help her out. Lunch in town at the Grub 'n' Go had been fun.

She couldn't believe she was enjoying her stay in town so far. She'd left Ragland because she wanted something more glamorous. In fact, she was missing out on what her friends were doing back in Nashville right now. Wasn't she?

High school, Mama, Nashville… It all seemed like forever ago. When she'd finally relented and agreed with Amanda to come home for the summer, she'd felt depressed at first. How was it that she felt more excited to get out of bed every morning now? Callie chuckled. Maybe it was Amanda's spaghetti.

But no. She knew the truth. It was Mark. He was still a wonderful person, albeit with a little extra baggage. She shook her head and put a hand on her stomach. There was no way there could ever be anything between them like before. Besides, he'd given her up once. He'd surely have no problem doing it again.

A light mist hung over the fields, but morning sunbeams broke through and lit up the world. Callie pulled into the gravel drive of the Pierce house and stopped to study it after parking the car. Something about it made her heart flutter. The fresh coat of paint and recently landscaped yard made it look idyllic, like a dream she'd once had but forgotten. She hopped out.

The hutch she'd bought from Mark was downstairs, but she hadn't seen it yet. Todd had dropped it off last evening as promised and put it inside the back door. She could work on it later on the enclosed back porch that had once been a butler's pantry.

She'd just started repositioning the twin beds after removing a hideous landscape painting from a wall when she heard a car door slam outside. Her ears perked up as the front door opened, and someone called out, "Cal, you here?"

"I'm up here, Amanda!" Callie trotted down the stairs.

"Hey, how are ya?" Her sister greeted her at the bottom step. She was looking around with a checklist in her hands. "This looks great. I like the sofa where you've positioned it. I could watch television and still see outside."

"Yep, that was my thought, too." Callie scanned the room. "I like the new picture over the mantel—at least, it's new to the house—and isn't the chandelier the cutest?"

"Too cute. What else do we need?"

Callie pointed up the stairs. "I've pretty much finished up except for the master bedroom. Once I find a bed, I already have some bedding I can use for staging, and then this place is ready to go."

"You're so talented." Amanda squeezed Callie's shoulder. "I could have never have done this. It looks like it's right out of a magazine."

Callie's cheeks warmed at the compliment. "Thank you," she sang. "It's all about the throw pillows." They both laughed. "Come on, let me show you the hutch."

Amanda followed her to the kitchen. They pushed open a glass-paned door that opened into what would become a mudroom.

"Wow," Amanda said, but she didn't sound impressed.

"Really? Look at it." Callie ran her hands down the side, admiring how smooth the finish was even after so many years.

"Todd said it was a piece of junk." Amanda

furrowed her brows. "I hope you paint it or something because that's not going to match at all."

"Not everything has to be matchy-matchy," argued Callie. "Besides…" she pulled open one of the drawers "…this fits the farmhouse. It was once beautiful, but it's had a little damage. With some hard work, it will be as good as new."

"If you say so," Amanda said.

Callie laughed. "I'll get to it this weekend or next, but you don't need to wait to list the house. Let's get a bed put in upstairs and put it on the market. I'll work on this in my free time and cover it up with a tarp for showings."

Amanda made a face. "I'd rather it be show ready."

"It will be. This room presents well enough. I'll get the hutch done in a couple weeks, and then you'll have everything perfect."

Amanda seemed wistful, but she nodded. They walked back into the kitchen and sat down in ladder-back chairs that surrounded a rustic planked table. Callie picked up her water bottle and unscrewed the cap.

"What are you doing on Saturday?" Amanda asked. "Do you want to come to the ball field in the morning? Justin has a game."

Callie started to agree, but she froze. Then

sheepishly admitted, "Actually, I'm going canoeing on Saturday."

"With who?" Amanda asked.

Callie's heart flipped in her chest, and she wondered why she felt the need to act like it was no big deal. "I'm going with Mark."

Amanda looked surprised.

Callie waved her hand like it was nothing. "When he picked me up the other day because you wouldn't answer your phone," she teased, "we went to lunch, and he mentioned he still had canoes at his parents' place."

"I'm sure he does."

"Yes, and he said we could go on Saturday."

"Wow." Amanda looked satisfied. "A date."

The words horrified Callie. "No, *not* a date." She forced herself to chuckle. "It's not a date, he's just a business associate and…" She hesitated. "I guess we're kind of friends again, but we're just hanging out."

"Hanging out." Amanda tossed her a look. "That's what you've been doing the past ten plus years in Nashville. It's called dating."

Callie shook her head in denial.

Amanda leveled her gaze like she was trying to send a message directly into Callie's brain. "I think Mark broke your heart. You keep complaining you can't find anyone, but you won't even commit to the idea of dating."

"I'm happy to commit. I just haven't met any-one serious, and I don't want to go through that again."

Amanda sat back with a sigh. "Mark's still a nice guy. You could do worse."

Callie knew that was the truth. "It didn't work out the first time, so I'm not going to let myself go there. I'm going canoeing, and he's going with me. Not a big deal. I promise."

Amanda looked away. "That big gaping hole in the kitchen needs a nice shiny refrigerator."

Callie glanced behind her, grateful for the change in subject. "Yeah, you said you ordered it, right?"

"I did last week, and it'll be here Monday." Amanda sighed. "It *should* be here Monday."

Callie beamed. "This house is going to be great. Wait and see. We'll get a big fat commission off of it."

"I hope so because I need it. I never knew kids were so expensive."

"I thought after the diaper phase, it was pretty much like having a pet."

"Not so much."

Callie said nothing, but the fleeting thought of motherhood skipped across the surface of her mind like a stone over water.

Would she ever have children of her own someday?

* * *

Callie was the last person Mark expected to see so soon. Back in high school, she'd been sweet and fun to talk to, but talking with her now was even better.

"I'm not here to bother you, I promise," she said. "It's just a business call."

Mark caught himself grinning. "You're not bothering me." He stood up from the shop's counter and put down the magazine he'd been thumbing through. "Are you looking for something?"

"Well, yes, but it's specific. I have the hutch in the farmhouse. It's going to look great when I get it finished."

"Good news."

"Yes, but I'm here because I still need a queen-or king-size bed frame for the farmhouse—fast. Can I see what you have?"

His eyes shifted across the store to where an assortment of headboards were stacked upright. He pointed. "Right over there. Come on, I'll show you."

A couple in shorts and Atlanta Braves baseball T-shirts stood in the front corner looking at some dishes. Taking some of Callie's earlier advice, he'd found some plate hooks and hung several of them on the wall with the price stickers showing on the outside.

Callie walked ahead of him, the back of her neck bare. She'd finally put her thick hair up into a ponytail.

A loud crash from the back made Mark wince. Just as Callie stopped, too, Hadley dashed to the front of the store through the center aisle, holding up her hands in surrender. She skidded to a halt in front of Callie in surprise.

Callie laughed. "Well, hi, there."

Studying her, Hadley smiled back, then she looked at Mark.

"What happened in the back?" He held his breath, afraid of what she'd say in front of Callie.

Her little cheeks flushed. "I knocked over the light. It's okay," she added in a rush.

"What light?"

"The gold light."

"The lamp?"

"Yes, on the floor. I didn't break it."

"Okay." Mark spoke calmly so she'd relax, and it worked. She looked back up at Callie. "Can you say hi to Miss Callie?"

"Hi, Miss Callie."

Callie dropped to her knees and folded her arms across them. "Hi, Hadley. It's nice to see you again. Are you working with your daddy today?"

Hadley nodded, then her face became solemn. "I can't go to school."

"Oh?"

Hadley glanced at Mark. He motioned toward the register. "Please go back to the counter and finish coloring your worksheet." To his relief, she skipped off.

Callie rose to her feet. The smile on her face eased his anxieties. Mark motioned toward the bed frames, his tongue tangled up in his thoughts.

Callie stepped over stacks of bed rails lying on the floor and started flipping through the headboards like she was going through a filing cabinet.

He stopped her at a queen-size headboard with a dark finish. "That piece is cherry. I bought it at an estate sale a few months ago. It's a nice size and an antique, too, most likely prewar."

Her eyes locked onto it as if processing some mysterious information he didn't have access to. "That could work. What do you want for it?"

He decided to be straightforward. He could use the realty company's business. "I paid thirty-five dollars for it, so I'd like to double my money. It's in good condition."

"Boy, you got it for a steal, didn't you?" She

held it by the post and examined the legs. "It has the footboard, right?"

He pointed to the smaller frame in front of it.

She hesitated. He expected her to haggle with him. "I need to make sure I get the best deal. Would you take sixty-five? I'll be in here often, and there are other Realtors in the area that I can recommend visit you."

"That'd be great, Callie. Deal." He held out his hand.

She gave it a swift shake, obviously pleased. "Now let me get out of here before I spend any more money. They have me on a per-project budget."

"Makes sense," he said. He headed toward the register, and she followed him. "So." He swallowed, trying not to be obvious as he took a steady breath. "Do you still want to go canoeing on Saturday?" He was embarrassed he'd waited so close to the weekend to bring up the canoe trip again, but he didn't want to make it sound like a date.

"Absolutely." Callie looked excited.

Straddling a yellow stool, Hadley looked up from her coloring. "I want to go!"

Callie didn't miss a beat. "That'd be so much fun," she replied, looking over at Mark for his approval.

"I like canoes," Hadley insisted.

Callie laughed. "Me, too. Has your daddy taught you how to paddle?"

"No."

"Now that's a shame." Callie gave Mark a teasing frown. "Every girl should have a canoe. Didn't you say that?"

He felt his smile widen. "I may have." They studied each other, and Mark realized Hadley coming along might be a good thing. He gave his daughter a serious look. "If she can be good tomorrow and not pull anyone's hair or throw things in class, she can come with us."

The little girl tossed her crayon onto the counter. "I won't pull Alexa's hair anymore," she promised.

Callie slanted her head at her. "That's a good promise to make. It's not nice to hurt other people."

Hadley's cheeks went pink. She quickly turned her attention to her worksheet and began folding it in crooked halves.

Callie glanced at Mark as he rang up her purchases. "A little trouble at school?"

"We've been asked to stay at home today."

"Oh, my."

Mark looked up at her amused face and accepted the credit card she held out. "We have a few behavior issues at pre-K."

"Hmm." Callie turned back to Hadley, who

had crumpled her worksheet into a ball. "Hadley, why did you pull Alexa's hair?"

Hadley held up the ball in her fist. "Because I was mad. She's mean."

"Why is she mean?"

"She has pretty hair and so does Natalie."

"I think you have pretty hair, too, honey."

Hadley pointed at her head, which Mark had managed to brush this morning but just barely. "I don't have braids."

"Do you like braids?"

"Girls have braids," Hadley said matter-of-factly. "But I don't."

Holding Callie's receipt in his hand, Mark stared at his daughter. This was all news to him.

Callie seemed to understand everything. "Do the other girls at school laugh at your hair?"

Hadley's eyes welled up with tears. "They said my hair's ugly."

"We don't get her hair brushed some days," Mark explained in a rush. He felt his cheeks go red in embarrassment.

"Ah," Callie said. "You can buy a detangler to make the brushing easier, and braiding is simple, by the way." She leaned down toward Hadley. "If you come canoeing with me on Saturday, I will braid your hair."

Hadley's eyes widened in surprise. Mark felt a lump in his throat. When Callie turned for her receipt, he pressed it into her hand. "Thanks," he murmured.

She grinned at him. "No problem. I'll see you Saturday. Where do you want to meet?"

Her enthusiasm was contagious. Mark hadn't been on the lake in several weeks and hadn't used any of the canoes in a couple years. "How about we just pick you up?" Her eyes sparkled, and he hoped he wasn't making it sound too much like a date. "I can throw a canoe in the back of the truck and swing by."

She started to nod but stopped. "Wait." She held up a finger. "Why don't I just drive to your house and help you load it? I can leave my car there."

"That sounds perfect." He could tell by her undisguised curiosity that she probably wanted to see the house again.

She looked out his store window. "Do you think we can get that headboard into my car?"

"Do your back seats lie down flat?"

She nodded.

"We'll get it in there. The sides will hang out the back, but I have some bungee cords."

"Perfect. Goodbye, Hadley. See you on Saturday."

Hadley was trying to smooth out her wrinkled worksheet. To Mark's surprise, she looked up at Callie and made eye contact. "Bye, Miss Callie!"

Chapter Seven

Callie woke up thirty minutes before her alarm went off on Saturday morning. After scarfing down a quick breakfast, she packed a water-proof drawstring bag with sunscreen, bug spray, cash and her driver's license, then threw in a couple of granola bars.

The drive took longer than she expected. Mark lived west of town in a dark brick house that sat an acre off of the road. Back behind the house, a large barn shone in the morning sun. Mark's pickup truck was parked just outside its doors. Hadley danced around in the truck bed.

Callie was just five minutes late, and he was already loading up. She walked past the house to his pickup truck. "Hi, Hadley."

The little girl's hair looked wet. She wore a pair of swim shorts and a pink princess shirt stained with purple marker or paint. Callie stopped at the side of the truck and leaned over the bed. "Are you ready to go canoeing?"

Hadley looked up, squinting hard in the bright sunshine. "I couldn't finish my cereal."

"I'm sorry to hear that."

"It was yucky!" she shouted.

Just then, Mark came stumbling out of the barn, pulling a long green canoe.

"Didn't you get that one at scout camp?" Callie asked him.

His hair was damp like he'd just washed it. "I think my father bought it from a sporting goods store outside Atlanta."

"Nice. Seems like you've always had it," Callie remarked. "Let me help you with that." She hurried past him and picked up the other end.

Mark heaved the front end up onto the tailgate of his truck and helped her slide the canoe into the back, dodging Hadley, who giggled with excitement. When he leaned down to pick up a life jacket he dropped, Callie coaxed Hadley into her arms, and she carried the child to the truck and let her climb into her car seat in the back.

Mark slammed the tailgate shut, and Callie hurried to the passenger side. He climbed in and looked over his shoulder to back out. "Are you ready?"

"Yes!" answered Hadley.

"Very." Callie couldn't help but smile. She remembered this truck. His father had driven it.

Rolling down her window, she breathed in the fresh air soaked with morning dew, late honeysuckle and the scent of leafy trees. "I love it down here," she murmured as they rolled west down the highway listening to a children's CD that kept Hadley's attention. Callie realized how much she'd missed home. Tennessee was beautiful country, too, but these Georgia lowlands were a part of her.

The wind whipped through the cab, blowing her hair all around her face and rippling the top of her shirt across her chest. She closed her eyes and almost felt seventeen again—carefree without any worries in the world. "I love summer, don't you?"

He glanced at her, then back to the road. "I do. It's my favorite season next to fall. I like the leaves turning colors."

"Same," Callie agreed. "I like summer best, though, because of the fireworks, watermelon, waterskiing, lightning bugs…"

"I used to dread summers as a kid," Mark said. "My dad had chores for me to do every morning. Now I have to do them on my own."

"I remember that! If you weren't at practice, he always had a project for you. Well, you have help now." She motioned to Hadley in the back seat and saw a faint smile tug at his jaw.

Callie stole a peek at his profile. He still looked like a baseball player, she thought. Tan and weathered, strong jaw, square chin, serious eyes.

"I still like being outside," he mused. "We used to have the twenty acres, but I sold some after Dad died to pay for funeral expenses." In a regretful tone, he added, "I sold off a few more a while back to update the house and fix the roof. I kind of wish I hadn't because I'm behind on rent for the Market now."

"Oh, you don't own that building?"

"No, I wish I did. My parents intended to buy it, but once they could afford it, it was no longer for sale. Matt McIntyre owns the whole north end of the square—the law office, my place and the salon."

Callie scrunched her brows. "Who's he?"

"He owns the bank."

Callie blinked at his curt tone. "McIntyre, right. I remember that name. It sounds like he owns half the town, too."

"Yeah, he does."

Callie made a mental note to remember that detail. If she had to approach the bank for a loan, it'd be good to know what she was getting into.

Mark turned up the music. He tapped his thumb on the steering wheel. Up ahead, a brown sign announced Walker's Lake.

Callie saw the shore from the distance through the lake's thick trees. "I love how clear the water looks. It's still green instead of ol' lake brown."

Mark chuckled. "We try to keep it clean."

"There's not a lot of waves today."

He motioned toward the full lot. "Boats went in early this morning, but they've moved on."

They parked and unloaded the canoe, then carried it down to the water's edge. Hadley pretended to help, and Callie convinced her to lift on her end.

While Mark went back to lock up the truck, Callie strapped on Hadley's life jacket. Small waves washed up over the pebbly shore and made a lapping sound. "Like this," she said, snapping the buckle on the little girl's safety gear.

"I wear this when I swim."

"You do? Are you a good swimmer?"

"Yes." In reply, Hadley dashed into the water but stopped ankle deep.

She looked back, and Callie smiled. "Stay right there so we don't forget to put you into the canoe with us." That seemed to do the trick.

Callie glanced toward the shore and saw Mark heading her way with a ball cap and glasses on.

He wore a T-shirt, athletic shorts and sports sandals. Her stomach did a cartwheel. She bit her lip and looked away.

In the distance, a bass boat floated in a cove, and the hum of a speedboat carried over the breeze as a skier flew across the surface of the water. "I've missed this."

Mark picked up the canoe and slid it into the shallows. Callie grabbed his forearm as she stepped in and reached for the sides to balance herself. "Front or back?" she asked.

"Up to you."

She grinned. "I'll steer first."

He let her have the stern and called for Hadley. She squealed with excitement and clambered in, rocking the boat so hard Callie squealed back and held on for dear life.

Laughing, Mark slipped the boat the rest of the way off the bank. Splashing into the lake with giant steps, he sloshed to the front of the canoe to climb in while Hadley wriggled with excitement. When they shoved off, Callie saw him look back at her over his shoulder, and her skipping heart graduated to backflips. She tried to put her thoughts in check. It was only friendship. Nothing more. Right?

Even as the sun began to warm up, Hadley's inquisitive chatter and Callie's good sense of direction and cheerful observations made the heat worth it. Mark pointed at a crane standing ankle deep on the shore.

"A bird!" shouted Hadley.

"He's beautiful," Callie called. She kept her strokes with the paddle even and strong, impressing him with her endurance.

"Are you getting tired yet?"

She laughed. "I tried to keep this up while living in Tennessee. There's lots of rivers and waterways there."

She drifted farther from the bank, moving into a current that carried them along. Another boat whisked by a few hundred yards away, and he watched the wake roll into waves and move their way.

"I like the waves," she warned, and they waited for them to hit. The canoe wiggled back and forth making Hadley cry out with nervous excitement, and Mark held her tight, enjoying the ride until it petered out. Callie splashed the paddle back into the water. "Do you want to switch up now?"

"Sure."

She paddled hard against the current toward a flooded alcove with tree stumps rising up out of the water. "I'm surprised we haven't seen any snakes."

He nodded. "We will. Of course, it's nothing like you see in the Gulf."

"How often do you go down to Florida these days?"

"I used to go two or three times a year. I'd rent a boat or go fishing sometimes."

"That sounds like fun. Do you still have coast guard buddies down there?"

"Yeah, we meet up now and then to go swimming and diving," Mark said.

"I was never much for swimming in the ocean."

He chuckled. "I remember. Your parents never let you go with me on spring break. It's the same as a lake, just deeper."

"Yeah, with waves and riptides and things that want to eat me."

Mark laughed as they reached the shallows. He jumped out and pulled the canoe onto the bank.

"I'm hungry," Callie said, and he agreed.

They found an overturned tree trunk lying in the grass nearby and plunked down on it under some shade while Hadley ran up and down the muddy shoreline.

Callie looked at her lap. "Oh, no. My legs are already sunburned."

Mark looked at her legs. They were pink. "You should put something on that before it gets any worse." He grabbed his knapsack and pulled out his sports drink. "Hadley, come take a drink."

"Gross," Callie said, elbowing him in the ribs, "how can you drink that warm?"

He laughed. "The same way you can drink that water," he said, motioning to the bottle in her hand.

Hadley came over, her hair hanging over her face. Mark handed her his drink.

"Hadley, would you like me to braid your hair now?" Callie asked.

The little girl stared like Callie was offering her a present.

"Here, turn around." Callie stood up behind her and smoothed her hair down with her fingers. She quickly made a loose braid that she tied with a hair band she'd worn around her wrist.

"That's beautiful," Mark said.

Callie took out her cell phone and snapped a picture and showed it to his little girl. Hadley couldn't stop touching the back of her head.

"That's my hair?"

"Yes," Mark said. "It looks awesome."

"It's a French braid," Callie explained.

"It's beautiful, honey," Mark said. "Here, finish this drink now."

Hadley ignored him and darted back off. Callie grinned and took another sip from her bottle, eyes studying the distant blue sky. "I've always loved it here. It's quieter than most places, and there aren't too many boats around."

"It'll pick up this afternoon, but you're right, there are more crowded places to be."

"You're lucky you still have this nearby."

He sat back and studied her. "You do, too."

She smiled. "For now. I wasn't sure I was going to like being back home."

"Why's that?"

Callie fell quiet for a few seconds, then said, "I really liked living in a city. I just…got home-sick once in a while."

Mark nodded. He'd felt that way in Florida.

"Not so much for home but just for the water and the trees and some place to go sit when you've had enough…" She waved her hand in the air. "Sometimes I just needed time alone with nature and God."

"You didn't visit your folks much."

She lifted a shoulder in a lazy shrug. "I came back every once in a while. Things just didn't get better with Mom."

"Why not?"

"Amanda was the good kid. I struggled in school keeping up with stuff." She sighed. "I figured it out eventually, though, what I needed to do to function."

He frowned and for some reason thought of

Hadley. "I'm sorry you went through that. I just thought of you as a happy-go-lucky kid."

"It's fine. Dad and I are good. He's disappointed I didn't move back in with him, but I don't want to be in a crowded neighborhood."

"I understand. That's why I joined the Coast Guard. I love the beach, and I wanted to see the world. I was burned out from baseball. I'd played since I was in kindergarten."

Callie nodded. She clearly remembered.

"It took over my life in high school." Mark wanted her to understand. "My parents pressured me to do well, and I did, but it all became too much."

"Why didn't you ever try the swim team?" Callie asked him.

"I thought about it, but I had to give it up for the baseball team. And to keep Dad happy."

Callie patted him on the back. "I never knew that. I guess that's what happens when you're so talented."

He made a sarcastic sound. "I wasn't that talented. It was just something I liked to do, so I worked hard at it—until it got to be too much."

"I'm sorry you were so overwhelmed. I hope I wasn't a part of that. I didn't realize the pressure you were under." She made a soft snorting sound. "No one had high expectations for me. That's Amanda's department."

Mark sat up, surprised at her self-deprecation. "Are you kidding? I haven't seen any of the houses you've staged, but I'm sure by the way your sister talks about you, they're amazing."

Callie's cheeks flushed. "I'll show you pictures of some houses I've staged some time."

"I'd like that."

Their eyes met, and his mind went blank. She seemed hesitant, and he wondered if she was trying to think of something to say or just remembering the past.

"I'm going to eat my granola bar now," she blurted. She fidgeted with the bag in her hands. "Want one?"

"No. Yes. Sure," Mark grimaced at his idiocy. He glanced up to see where Hadley was. She was throwing handfuls of mud, and her shirt was smeared with it.

He watched Callie unwrap the granola bar and realized sadly that she wasn't interested in him in the old way anymore. The last thing she needed was a guy like him—a man with no big-city ambitions—hiding out in an antiques shop with ancient furniture, creepy dolls and a motherless child.

Sunday morning Callie decided to go to church. She made it on time and sat with her sister's family, squeezed in between Justin and Nicole. Then she noticed Mark sitting in the back with Hadley and an older couple. Trying not to appear nosy, she turned back to the service.

Afterward, Callie made her way down the aisle to say hello. Hadley jumped up on the pew and opened her arms wide like she expected a hug. Everyone stared, so Callie gave the little girl a squeeze. Her hair was knotty and slipping out of a soft terry hair band.

"Callie, this is Frank and Lois Ridley," Mark said, motioning toward the couple beside him. "Lois babysits Hadley for me when she's not minding the store."

"Ah," Callie said. "I was hoping to run into you sometime, at the store, I mean." She gave Mark a teasing grin. "There's a set of spoons I'm very interested in."

Mark must have told Lois and her husband the story because they both laughed. The woman shook her head. "Those spoons were Mark's mother's pride and joy. They came all the way from Rhode Island after the Civil War."

"It's a long story," Mark added.

Suddenly Hadley clutched onto his shoulders. "I'm hungry, Daddy."

"We better get you some lunch," Lois declared.

"I just wanted to say hi," Callie said with a chuckle. Lois took Hadley by the hand and led her away. Callie turned to Mark. "And thanks again for yesterday," she added.

His eyes brightened. "I had fun. I mean, we had fun, Hadley and I." He glanced up at the dwindling crowd and nodded to Gabby from the diner.

"I was up all night watching hair-braiding videos," he confessed.

"You were?" For some reason, Callie found that endearing.

"I'm going to practice on her tonight if she'll let me."

"I suspect she will." Callie glanced toward the door where Hadley had disappeared. "I remember getting into trouble a lot as a kid, and no one ever asked me for an explanation—a real one."

"I'm glad you pointed that out." Mark looked at her with serious eyes. "I had no idea kids were being mean to her because of her hair, I just thought it was because, you know…"

"She's pretty active," Callie agreed. "Don't be surprised if she takes a while to adjust to school. Just be patient."

He nodded. "Thanks."

"No, thank you. I had a great time yesterday, and she's a cutie."

Mark let a small smile escape. "You just think so because she hasn't flushed anything down your pipes yet."

They parted, and Callie hurried over to Amanda's house to help with lunch. It'd felt nice to go to church. It had been even better to see Mark there. Amanda had told her he seldom came, usually sending Hadley with her sitter.

Callie sighed, washing out a pot in the sink. "Why don't you just make sandwiches for lunch? No wonder you're tired all the time."

Amanda laughed. "Todd and the kids eat sandwiches all week long."

Callie grudgingly admired her dedication. Filling the pot with water for pasta, she gazed out the window at the kids' hound dog in the backyard. Buster was chasing a butterfly as he loped across the yard like an antelope. She chuckled. "Your dog is nuts."

"That's why he fits in." Amanda stirred a pot of cheese, eggs and sour cream on the stove for homemade mac and cheese. "So, how'd yesterday go? You said you'd tell me later."

Callie turned off the faucet and leaned back against the sink. "It was a lot of fun actually, but it wasn't a date. He brought Hadley."

"Uh-huh."

"Seriously, it wasn't."

Amanda smiled and stuck out her tongue. "Did he open the door for you?"

"Nope."

"Did he help you in and out of the water?"

Callie rolled her eyes. "He's a gentleman."

"Good listener?"

"Of course. You already know that."

"How'd he look?"

"What do you mean, how'd he look? He looked like himself."

"Did you all swim?"

Callie turned back to the sink to hide her cheeks. They felt warm. "Yeah, we swam a little. Right before we went back to the truck. It was so hot I just jumped into the middle of the lake, then he helped me back in, and we took turns with Hadley."

"Hmm…"

"Not a big deal."

"So no sweet talk for old times' sake?"

Callie burst into laughter. "With a child there? No. We just talked. I told you, we're just friends now." She plopped the pot onto the stove, and water splashed back onto her arms. "If I want to find a date, I'll use my dating app."

Amanda laughed. "It didn't do you any good in Nashville. Just try it the old-fashioned way."

"It works for lots of people, and besides, I was too busy trying to do something with my life."

Amanda poured dry macaroni into the boiling water. "Don't be so hard on yourself."

Callie forced a smile. "I thought I'd have a

successful shop by now instead of trying to hold down a job."

"You've only been here a few weeks," Amanda reminded her, "and we've already sold a house that you went through and suggested changes."

Callie was pleased in spite of herself. "Yeah, but I haven't had any time to look at any more commercial spaces or run any numbers."

"You're doing great. With all that land on the Pierce property, we needed the farmhouse to look fabulous to justify the price. It looks amazing."

"Drab to fab," Callie agreed. "All I have left to do is refinish the hutch."

"Awesome. I'm going to go ahead and get it listed this week."

"Perfect. I could use the cash."

"Now," Amanda said, "do you still have feelings for him or what?"

Callie found herself staring into the almost boiling water. "I could," she said. "I mean, I loved him once." She heard Amanda's sharp intake of breath and waved the spoon at her. "Don't go there. He's a heartbreaker. It would just end up not working out. It'd be a disaster, and I'd be the girl who got dumped by Ragland's golden boy. Twice!"

Amanda moved to the sink and started washing a mixing bowl. Her silence made Callie try to believe she could never love Mark again, even if deep down inside she knew it'd be easy.

"He's no heartbreaker, I can tell you that. He just doesn't have a whole lot of faith in people." Amanda's voice sounded thoughtful.

Callie could see that. "Well, I know something happened between him and Hadley's mother, but he acts like he let the whole town down because he didn't go to the minor leagues."

"Ancient history. Nobody talks about that anymore." Amanda rinsed the bowl and set it on the sideboard to drain. "He doesn't date much, you know. If he does, it never lasts."

For some reason, this made Callie feel strange relief. "I hope he doesn't think I wasted my life moving to Nashville instead of hanging around and waiting on him."

"You didn't, Callie, and don't worry, you're still the kind of woman he needs."

There was an hour before he had to be at the Antique Market Monday morning, so Mark walked down the driveway to get the weekend's mail. He'd planned to take Hadley into her class and sit with her awhile to observe, but they were running late. The air smelled like honeysuckle. He reached the mailbox and flipped the lid down, expecting nothing. There was a flyer for the hardware store and two white envelopes.

He pulled his pocketknife out to slit one open as he walked back up to the house. He opened it expecting to see McIntyre's signature. It was a form letter. Frowning, he read the late bill notice. They'd sent him one last month even though he'd called, and again for June, even though he'd tried to explain his situation out already. Frustrated, he crumpled the letter and envelope into a stiff ball.

McIntyre would be at the ball field tomorrow night, probably with his team. Maybe he needed a long, detailed explanation in person. Sales were down since Christmas. There'd been unexpected expenses. Trying to maintain a small business on the town square was a challenge, especially with the high rent McIntyre was charging this year.

After leaving Hadley at school, Mark headed over to the Grub 'n' Go for a late breakfast. He grabbed a biscuit from the take-out counter and maneuvered through the crowd, nodding hello to Mrs. Bake from the florist shop and the other shop owners. He'd almost made it out of the store when someone called his name.

Lois stood in the back of the line, motioning at him. He hurried up beside her.

"Did Hadley make it to school?"

"Yes," Mark said with a sigh of relief. "I used the tangle spray you gave me and managed a simple braid, and she was happy enough with that."

"That's good." Lois lifted her readers off her nose. "Did you talk with her about pulling hair and throwing things?"

"I didn't see the point of doing that again. We talked this weekend. I mean I really talked to her and tried to ask the right questions."

"I'm sure she'll be okay."

"I hope so."

Lois shook her head. "No, I don't mean right away. It's going to take time. She has to learn how to make friends and how to control her temper."

"Right," agreed Mark.

"Don't worry. She'll grow out of this with a little direction."

"Thanks." The line moved up, and he walked beside her. "Can I buy your breakfast?"

"No," Lois said with a smile. "By the way, where is your friend today?"

Mark forced a chuckle and looked away.

"It's okay," his mother's old friend said gently. "You can have a life and a little girl, too."

He shrugged. "I'm busy. I have the store to worry about, and I do play on the softball team."

"I know." Lois smirked. "But that's not the

life I'm talking about. You know she's praying for her now."

"Who?"

"Hadley. Every time she says prayers, she asks for a mommy instead of a cat."

Mark felt his face flush. "She's added that lately."

"Who knows if it's been on her mind even before that?"

It pained him to think his daughter already felt like there was a hole in her life.

Lois patted his arm. "The Lord works in mysterious ways."

Mark forced a smile, waved goodbye and hurried out. Hadley was a precocious child. She couldn't possibly mean anything with her prayers. She hardly knew Callie at all. And why would Callie ever consider giving him a second chance after what he'd done to her?

That ship had sailed a long time ago.

Chapter Eight

Callie made it to the Pierce farmhouse by nine on Monday morning. The cool air felt refreshing, and she enjoyed every breath of it because she knew the day would heat up fast. The yard smelled like fresh-cut grass, and the breeze carried something sweet on it along with the chatter of birds.

She did a final walk-through of the house, satisfied that everything was in place. The new bed frame was set up in the master bedroom, and a gas stove and fridge stood in the kitchen.

She'd filled an old milk pitcher with dried wildflowers and baby's breath and positioned it in the middle of the dining table and its place settings. It looked like a breakfast dream with the windows casting lovely rays of early morning sunshine into the room. She walked over and opened one of the windows to freshen the stale air. A wonderful breeze whooshed inside.

Setting her purse and keys on the counter, Callie walked to the back porch. Against a wall, the hutch was covered with a canvas tarp. She pulled it off and got to work.

After thirty minutes, she'd toted in her supply box from the car, wiped down the hutch with a damp cloth, dried it and removed most of the hardware. All that was left was to pull out the drawers and remove the two lower cabinet doors.

Crouching down, Callie breathed in the pleasant smell of old wood finish like good medicine. She eased out the left drawer and peered inside. To her surprise, the drawer track was made of wood instead of metal, but it still looked solid. It would at least need to be tightened down.

She wiped out the drawer opening with her dust cloth, then turned to the second drawer. It came out most of the way but got stuck before she could get it all the way out. She pulled gently, but it refused to budge. She wiggled it, and it gave a little.

She wiggled a little harder and tugged forward. After squinting into the cracks to see, Callie stood up and jiggled the drawer up and down. It finally surrendered, and she eased it out, hoping she hadn't bent the track or broken the slide.

The drawer fell into her hands, and she flipped it over and looked at the bottom. It appeared a little marked up, but not too bad. It'd caught on something.

She squatted back down and stuck her hand into the dark space. The edges of the track were smooth. It did feel a little sideways, definitely not straight. Frowning, she saw something against the hutch's back and reached for it. It looked like a piece of silverware.

Callie closed her fingers around a smooth, cool spoon and pulled it out triumphantly.

This was no ordinary piece of flatware. The spoon looked tarnished, which meant it could be silver. She studied the delicate etching marks that framed the handle and the curious dip of the mouth. Turning it over, she noted a maker's mark.

Mark's spoon rack at the shop flashed in her mind. Maybe she could sell it to him… No, that wouldn't be right. It'd been in the hutch he'd sold to her.

She waffled back and forth about what was fair, then tossed the spoon into her supply box and made a mental note to deal with it later. At the very least she could keep it as a good luck charm. When she went back to check her phone messages, she saw that Amanda had not called after all.

Hitting the playback button, Callie listened to her boss explain there were some Realtor classes he'd like her to take and ask her to get back to the office as soon as possible to meet with another one of his real estate agents. She texted him, then grabbed her purse. She locked the house up behind her, frustrated she hadn't done more on the hutch. But until she had her own business, she was at someone else's mercy.

Tuesday and Wednesday it rained, and soft-ball practice was moved to later in the week. Business at the shop was brisk early in the week, and Mark felt a surge of hope. Slowly, but surely, he was catching up with the Antique Market's late rent. The problem was, it wasn't fast enough.

Monday morning a woman in a business jacket and narrow skirt strode into the shop with a list in her hand. She scanned the room, then saw him at the counter and gave him a profes-sional smile—brisk and tight. Curious, he let her come to him.

She walked over without a wobble on her high heels. Before she even reached the counter, her hand extended in greeting. "Melanie Roberts."

He took her hand, mind racing to remember if he should know her.

"Callie mentioned me? Callie Hargrove?"

He hesitated, trying to recall if Callie had or not. "I'm sorry," he said with a small chuckle because Melanie Roberts's stare looked as expectant as her arrival. "She may have, but I'm not sure."

The lady clucked her tongue. Her hair was up in a loose bun that may have been fashionable on some women, but it made her look like a cranky seventh-grade English teacher. "I'm not surprised. Callie hasn't returned my emails since Sunday."

"I'm sure she's just busy," Mark said in her defense. Callie wasn't one of those people who spent all of her time on her phone, she was just distracted easily. Kind of like Hadley. "What can I do for you?"

"Well," Melanie said, "I'm with Deep South Realty in Burlington, and Callie said you had some nice bed frames."

"That I do," Mark replied. He came around the counter and motioned with his arm across the room but let the lady lead. Once she had the bed frames in her sights, she made a beeline, marching over things in the way without even looking. She slipped the paper in her hand under her arm and started sorting through the frames without his help or encouragement.

"Any size in particular?" he asked.

Melanie nodded but didn't reply. He waited. She seemed to know what she wanted. Right when he was going to return to the counter, she stepped back and took a lingering look at the long rails stacked on the floor that went with the headboards. "I'll take the king there with the cherry finish, and all the twin beds you have."

Mark blinked in surprise, then realized she was waiting for him to respond. "Okay, that's great."

Before he could say anything else, she said, "I won't haggle you over price, but can I get some kind of bulk discount?"

Mentally counting the twin beds he had, he replied, "I have three sets of twin frames. I can do fifteen percent off." The king bed he'd marked up, and he'd bought it for a steal.

She gave a sharp nod. "That'll do. I have two empty houses to fill. You deliver, right?"

The Antique Market occasionally delivered, more like personal favors for neighbors and friends, but Mark realized his reply could make or break the deal.

"Sure, yes," he said, grateful he'd never traded the truck in for something with better gas mileage. Times were changing. People were busy. His mind raced to recall Jake's schedule for future reference should he ever be asked to deliver something heavier than bed frames.

"That's perfect. I'm actually on the far side of Burlington, so it'll be close to an hour drive. We'll cover gas."

Mark exhaled, careful not to let it come out as a sigh, and licked his lips, thinking. "Well then, I can deliver after hours during the week or in the morning on Saturday."

Melanie looked pleased. "I work until seven. Can you drop them off by tomorrow then?"

"Sure." He gave her his most charming smile and held out his hand.

Her brittle facade softened, and she shook his hand.

"I'll check you out at the counter," he added.

She gave a swift nod and waited while he pulled the tags off the bed frames she wanted. He rang it all up and even with the discount, it came to just under four hundred dollars. She didn't blink an eye, and he cheered silently at his success in connecting with an agent at one of the biggest realty companies in the region.

After she took her leave, he added the sale to the books and started all over again, admitting it was time to use a computer program instead of his father's old register with crisp, aging pages. If he started charging a delivery fee, it'd bring in a little bit more cash. Callie sending Realtors his way was an enormous help, and he didn't have any more valuable collections to sell. Besides the spoons.

A familiar country song began to play on the speakers overhead, and the singer said something about his girl, his gift. Mark smiled. Callie Hargrove might not be his girl anymore, but she was certainly a gift and an answer to his unspoken prayers.

Tuesday morning, a sharp knock on Callie's office door made her jump. Her boss, Mr. Martin, strode in with a terse face. She sat up straight. "Have you been out to the farmhouse lately?"

She shook her head. "Not since yesterday."

"I just got a call. A window was left open, and it rained inside the house."

The window! Her mind whirled.

Mr. Martin threw up his hands. "We just listed this thing Monday afternoon, Callie." His voice rose, and she saw the frustration, and worse, the accusation in his eyes.

"Well," she admitted, "I was there for the final walk-through before the listing and to work on a showpiece in the back."

"Did you open the window?"

Callie hesitated.

"How many showings have we had?" He glared.

She bent over the keyboard and typed in a few phrases. "Just the one, this morning," she said, trying to look somewhat cheerful. They'd scheduled a showing in the first week.

He exhaled. "You must have opened a window." His eyes flickered with barely controlled anger. "No one has been in the house since you, and the agent who showed it this morning called Amanda and told her the floors were wet."

Callie took a deep breath. "You're right," she said, talking fast before his head exploded. "It was stuffy in there, and I opened a window in the dining area."

He put his hands on his hips and glared at her. Jumping up from her chair, Callie held out a hand like a stop sign. "Don't worry about it, I'll get right over there. The floors are probably dry already."

He gave her a hard look. "It rained all night. I have a limb down in my front yard from the wind."

Callie tried to look sympathetic and totally in control at the same time. "Don't fret, I'm on my way. I was going to work on the hutch anyway."

He gave her a sharp nod. "Well, you're going to be working on the floors now, and I need it done by tomorrow."

Callie forced herself to give him a meek smile and cleared her throat. "Yes, sir. I'll head right over." Her stomach slunk down into her shoes until she felt like she was going to throw up. "On my way," she repeated, hurrying past him in the doorway.

It wasn't until she got into the car that she remembered he said the people looking at the house had called Amanda. Resentful, she peeled out of the parking lot and around the square.

The Antique Market was on her way, and the memory of the long conversation she'd had with Mark on the phone last night washed over her, helping her panic ebb. He'd called to thank her for telling Melanie Roberts about the shop, and they'd ended up talking for almost an hour. She said she owed him lunch for the canoe trip, and he insisted her business referral more than paid for it.

"At least somebody thinks I'm getting it right," she said out loud. The cars in front of her braked, and she stopped. Through the passenger window, she saw she was directly in front of the Antique Market's front door. With an impulsive twitch, she waited for traffic to continue, then pulled into a tight parking spot and hopped out. If anyone in town knew anything about water damage, Mark would.

She hurried into the shop. Mark stood on a

two-step ladder, wiping off the tops of the picture frames hung along the wall in front of the pile of bedroom furniture.

Breathless, Callie called, "Hey!" and he looked over his shoulder. "Nice feather duster," she added, unable to resist teasing him despite the urgency of the situation. "Is Hadley at school today?"

"So far."

Stopping herself from sighing with relief, she gushed, "I need a favor," as he stepped down from the ladder.

"Oh, yeah, what's that?" His easy, unruffled demeanor felt instantly soothing.

"I messed up." She swallowed down a shard of tension in her throat.

"What happened?" Mark tossed the bright blue feather duster aside and strode over to meet her. His indigo eyes widened with concern.

"I left a window open at the farmhouse." Callie felt tears coming but held them back. She took a deep breath. "I opened a window yesterday while I was at the Pierce house. I was working on that hutch and got a phone call and had to leave, so I did, thinking I'd get back later. I mean," she rushed on, "I left my tools and everything. I meant to go back, I just haven't had time, and I didn't realize I'd left the window open."

Mark finally put it together. "And it rained last night."

"Yes, and from the sound of it, it poured into the house." Callie grimaced. "I was hoping… I—I thought…"

"I'll come out and have a look," he said. It was like he'd read her mind. She almost jumped into his arms but restrained herself. Instead, she clasped her hands and held them to her chest.

"Oh, please. If there's any damage, I have no idea how I'm going to be able to get it fixed before the next showing."

"Don't worry," he said, moving past her to the counter. "It's almost my lunch anyway. I was going to lock up for an hour. Let me call Lois and see if she can come in after lunch, and I'll ride with you out there and have a look."

"That would be awesome. Thank you so much, Mark." She felt her eyes water. "I'm hoping there's no major water damage. I could really use a second opinion."

"We'll see," he said in a matter-of-fact tone. He locked up the register, and Callie went to the front door to wait. Relief lifted the weight off her shoulders. He went to the back and returned carrying an old toolbox and a crumpled grocery bag. "Let's go."

Callie pushed the door open with determination. On the way to the Pierce farm, Callie explained that the house had just been listed. "We had a showing this morning, and the agent from another company was kind enough to call it in."

"That was good of her."

"Him," corrected Callie. "I can't remember his name, but I think we've met. Mr. Martin has a luncheon every quarter where he invites real estate agents from all over to come and network, and of course, to pass out flyers of our listings."

"Smart man. Is that where you met Melanie Roberts?"

"Yes." Callie kept her eyes on the road as they headed to the house. "I met several people and a few asked me about staging. That's when I mentioned your shop."

"You have no idea how much I appreciate that."

"You're welcome. I'm surprised you don't do that kind of thing already."

"Oh, no," he said, tapping his fingers along the side of the passenger door. "My parents just ran the shop. They didn't worry about marketing and advertising back then. Their idea of an ad was paying a couple of dollars to be in the local newspaper."

Callie glanced over and smiled. "Times have changed."

"Right," Mark agreed. "I realize it's time I start a website."

Callie nodded and sped down the highway like a madwoman until they came upon the Pierce property. She slowed down so she didn't send Mark flying into the dashboard when she careened into the driveway. A giant white realty post stood in the center of the yard. Her sister's name and face were on the small sign hanging beneath it.

"You must be proud of her," Mark said as they climbed out of the car.

"Yes, I am." As they climbed the porch stairs, she added, "But I'm not so sure it's the other way around."

He chuckled as they passed through the door into the house. "You're awfully hard on yourself. She and Todd talk about you like you hung the stars."

The metaphor made her smile.

"Come on," he said, "show me this window."

Callie's steps slowed as she walked into the kitchen. Mark walked around the table first and looked at the floor. She could see, even from where she stood, that the floor was different colors. Her heart pinched. The drywall under the window was wet, too.

He crouched down to look at the floor more closely. "It's just a few boards."

Callie walked around the table and stopped behind him. She let her hand rest on his shoulder. "Oh, no," she groaned. "They're swollen. Look how they're all raised up." She put a hand to her heart. "Mr. Martin's going to kill me."

Mark reached for her hand, holding it in his to comfort her. "He's not going to see it, is he?"

She hesitated. "He said I have to get this fixed by tomorrow."

Mark's expression fell. He let go of her fingers and scratched his neck. "That's a tall order." He looked down and studied the floor, then pushed the table and chairs back.

Callie huffed. "I can dry out the wall and windowsill with a hair dryer and touch them up if I need to, but there's no way I could get the flooring out here before next week, even if I laid it myself. That's it. I'm done. They're going to fire me so fast I'll drive out of here in flames."

Mark gave a soft laugh. "You aren't going to get fired, honey. I've got stacks of wood from old houses in the back of the store we can match up. I'll cut them, and we can sand them down and stain them if you have some stain left over."

Conflicted, Callie hesitated. "I can refinish floors, I know how to do that. I just need the pieces and the… Well, I don't know what to do about what's underneath, but I can stain them."

"Sounds like a team effort." Mark eyed her seriously, but it was a question, too.

"I can't take you away from your business

just to save myself." She closed her eyes. Her dream of a boutique seemed to be even further out of reach. "I needed this temp job. I know I need to answer for my own absentminded mistakes, but I need this job to have some money for the boutique, or else it's back to Nashville and working for someone else."

He nodded in understanding. "It's no problem. I had a delivery I can move to tomorrow night. Lois is minding the store until closing, and if I open a little late in the morning, no big deal."

Callie laughed dryly. "Business is that slow on the square?"

"For some of us. The cleaners on the corner closed up, but for others, things have picked up with all of the growth."

She sighed. "What about Hadley?"

Mark looked around the farmhouse. "If you don't mind her running around in here while we work, I'll have Lois pick her up and drop her off after the Market closes."

Callie closed her eyes. "God bless Lois."

"I know," Mark agreed. "She's all I have."

"I have no choice but to take you up on this, and I'll owe you big time—you're a lifesaver."

Mark frowned at her. "Seriously, hasn't anyone ever done anything for you without expecting something in return?"

Her laugh was doused in sarcasm. "No. Well," she relented, "maybe my sister, but…nope. She got me the job, and I'm her official babysitter now."

Mark smiled. "Let me have your keys, and I'll head back to the shop and get the replacement boards. You stay here, move this stuff out of the way and start removing the ruined pieces, if you know how."

She arched a brow at him. "I know how. I helped Dad lay wood floors in our house."

He winked. "Then you're a pro."

She watched him leave, thankful for his help. When she heard the car start up outside, she wiped her eyes and pressed her fingers to her forehead. Operation Salvage Callie was underway.

It was by far the best all-nighter Mark could remember having in a long time. He and Callie worked as a team, cutting, staining and replacing the boards while taking turns running with Hadley, who played hide-and-seek upstairs until she fell asleep on the couch.

Callie stood back a few feet, admiring their work. Her hair was up in a high ponytail with strands that had worked their way loose throughout the night. Makeup had faded, giving her face a natural, outdoorsy look, except for the dark smudges under her eyes from lack of sleep. When she spoke, her voice sounded raspy.

"That looks amazing. It's hardly noticeable."

Mark pushed the plastic sheeting with brushes and stain cans away from the drying floorboards and leaned back on his hands. "When it dries, the stain will be lighter. No one will ever know."

Callie leaned back and folded her arms. "How long do you think I should wait until I seal it?"

He glanced back to study her. She looked much calmer than she had yesterday when she'd rushed into the shop on the verge of panic. "I'd wait about two days," he suggested. "Don't you think?"

She nodded in agreement, then joined him, collapsing onto the floor beside him. Her black trousers were ruined, with a small hole above one knee and several sticky swipes of dark maple-colored wood stain. "I can't thank you enough for this. I had absolutely no idea how I was going to get this repaired in twenty-four hours. He asked the impossible."

Mark shook his head, staring at the floor. "Maybe he didn't realize how much damage there was."

"Or maybe he doesn't know what it takes to lay floors."

The house fell silent. They'd turned off the

music they'd sang all night to keep themselves
awake. He reached down and patted her hand,
and she caught his fingers with her own, so he
left it there. He cleared his throat. "We got it
done. I can't think of any reason they can't show
the house today if they have a request."

"Yep, except it still smells like pizza in here."
She broke into exhausted giggles.

He sniffed. "I can't believe we ate two piz-
zas."

She kept laughing, then fell backward,
sprawled out on the floor and put her hands
over her face as the laughter spilled out. Tears
trickled down her temples and into her hair.

That made him start laughing and after a
while he reached out and tapped her leg. "Stop
it. You're going to put us both out of our minds."

"Sorry, I'm sleep deprived," she gasped between giggles. She tried to regain control but
only managed sniffs and swallows before breaking into guffaws again when their eyes met.

Wiping her eyes and taking deep breaths,
Callie managed to sit up as far as leaning on
her elbows. "You're at your shop as much as
I'm at the office."

"Actually, Lois covers on Saturdays, and I
don't open on Sundays."

"Why is that?"

He shrugged. "That's the way my parents

did it." He took a breath. "That's something I'll never change. I'm not going to compromise my values—even to save a store."

She studied him. "So," she said, drawing up her knees and wrapping her arms around them, "how bad is it really? The store, I mean."

Mark tried not to sigh. "They raised the rent in January, and I've had a hard time keeping up. The first quarter of the year is never a great one, and I was late on my April payment."

He wondered how much more he should tell her. Last night, she'd told him about her bad luck with dating, the not-so-great financial choices she'd made and the regrets she had never making peace with her mother. All he'd talked about was baseball and high school.

He took a deep breath. "Actually, I missed May, too, but I just sent in half. I sold off my baseball card collections, so I'm hoping to catch up with June by the first week of July." He exhaled. "To be honest, I feel like everything's turning to sand and streaming through my fingers. I can't get a hold of it."

Her face smoothed out in sympathy.

Mark leaned forward and crossed his legs. "I've spent most of my life trying to make up for letting my parents down by not playing baseball professionally, and if I lose this store, I'll feel like a failure again. Plus, there really isn't anything else I want to do. I enjoy going to auctions and yard sales—like you. Cleaning things up and finding them a new home feels like I'm carrying on someone's story. Plus…" he grinned, because she already knew this "…I like collecting baseball cards and old toys and junk."

She raised a brow. "And dollies."

She was so funny. "And old dolls when people bring them to me, but Hadley enjoys them."

Callie laughed and leaned forward. "Maybe you should just focus on what sells best and think about updating the store."

"What do you mean?"

Her golden tawny eyes went wide. "Bring it into this century. All of the inventory looks like it's been dropped anywhere. I can tell you've tried to put similar things in the same areas, but an old desk covered with two hundred candlestick holders doesn't quite work. Have you thought of setting up displays? Little mini rooms or scenes with themes from the same era?"

Mark's mind could suddenly see the old school desk set up by the front window with a few of his prized tin lunch boxes on it, with a shelf of toys and framed autographed sports cards. "I've never really thought seriously about it. I assumed people like to dig through things. I mean, I do."

"A lot of people do, but this would make it

easier. Just going into the shop is a dig. Most collectors visit several stores in one day, right?"

"I'm sure some do." She was making sense. Just the way she'd cleaned up and presented this old farmhouse showed how she could see the big picture. Had she always been able to do that? Should he have moved to Nashville way back when?

Callie gazed up through the windows over the dining area. The sun had risen. "You're lucky. I always wanted my own place, a little shop that sells refinished furniture and candles and textiles. You know, pretty things."

"Old things made new?"

"Yes." A rooster crowed in the distance, and they could hear it even with the windows shut. "It's so peaceful out here."

He watched her, his heart keeping time along with his breathing and the quiet hum of the house. "This place is only four miles from the lake."

"Oh? Are we that close?"

Mark nodded. "Do you want to clean up and go for a drive after I drop Hadley off at school?"

They agreed to take Callie's car after driving it and the truck back to Mark's house. Callie knew she would be late for work, and she didn't care. Mr. Martin had left another message about attending a real estate license class, and she wasn't interested. Instead, she listened with interest as Hadley showed her the odd collections around her room: a bird's nest, a beach pail filled with rocks, a crumpled butterfly, dolls with missing arms and legs—and hair.

"Are you ready yet?" Mark called out.

Callie pretended to gasp, and it stopped Hadley in her tracks. "We better hurry. Let's get you dressed super fast!"

The little girl laughed.

"She's almost ready!" Callie called into the hall.

Moving as fast as she could, she changed Hadley into a pair of shorts hidden at the bottom of a dresser and found a pretty shirt hanging in the closet with the tags still on. Seating Hadley on her bed, Callie brushed out her hair with only a minor struggle, then made a dainty waterfall braid on one side of her head and pulled the rest back into a ponytail.

Hadley stared. "It's pretty."

"If you think it is," Callie said firmly. "You should wear your hair the way *you* like it."

The girl glanced up at her in surprise, and Callie figured that was a talk for when she was a little older. "If you go brush your teeth and beat me to the car with your backpack, I'll take you canoeing again if your daddy says it's okay."

Hadley jumped to her feet and raised her fists into the air. "Okay!"

Callie laughed and made sure to lose the race.

After dropping Hadley off at a small clapboard building just a half mile from the square and across the street from the elementary school, Mark came back out to her car, put the car seat into the hatchback and dove into the driver's side.

"Ready?"

Callie nodded and rolled the window down, thankful he felt like driving because she didn't. The air smelled like damp grass and warm sunshine on pavement. Her belly was full of pizza and flat soda, but she still felt content. She'd washed her face in the kitchen sink at the farmhouse and brushed her hair out before putting it back up.

Mark rolled down his window, too, and she dug around under the seat for her white baseball cap that read Music City.

"I haven't been out to the lake since we went canoeing," she said, "but I've been meaning to."

"I took Hadley fishing after church on Sunday."

"That was sweet of you."

He seemed to appreciate the compliment, but he kept his eyes on the road and hummed along to the radio. Callie studied his profile and the tired lines under his eyes. Birds made a cacophony in the passing power lines. Soon, the lake became visible through the woods.

They pulled into one of the small parks around the lakeshore, and Mark motioned toward a trailhead through a grove of trees. "There's the old walking trail that loops around the water if you want to go for a little hike."

"Let's go." Excited to be out of the house, Callie locked the doors to her car when he tossed her the keys. They passed into the cool shade of a tree canopy with clumpy water plants growing up the small embankment next to the woods.

Their hands swung, close enough to touch, and Callie felt self-conscious. She'd walked the trails with Mark before but under much different circumstances.

"You still love it here," he observed.

"I do."

Callie suddenly wanted Mark to hold her hand, but she forced herself to keep walking and not think about it. He'd broken up her with a lifetime ago. It was over.

A breeze rippled across the lake's surface, then drifted through the trees. A warm flood of peace washed over her. "I went to a lake outside of Nashville a lot. By myself most of the time, but I never felt quite safe."

Mark nodded. "It's still safe here." He touched

her hand in midswing, and she caught his fingertips as they clasped hands. Callie's heart gave a pleasant lurch.

"How long do you think you'll keep the Market open?" She forced herself to speak calmly and not to stutter like a flustered schoolgirl.

"Oh, it'll be a while. As long as I can work or until Hadley takes it over if she wants," he answered in a soft voice.

"Then a Florida vacation home?"

Mark's intense gaze drank in the green-blue lake water in the distance. "Maybe. That's the plan for the future. Nothing's set in stone."

"Hmm," Callie said. She wondered what would happen to the store. It'd be an amazing space for a charming boutique—not that she could afford it right now. "Antique stores are a Southern staple. Maybe you'll never go out of business."

Mark gave a faint chuckle. "Not if the bank has their way."

She felt bad for him. She knew what it was like to struggle to stay afloat. "You have so much inventory," she said, then thought of the spoons. "There's probably a lot you could get rid of and just slowly replace with better stuff. I mean, if it doesn't sell, why keep it?"

"I guess," he mused.

"What about the spoons?"

He shifted his gaze from the treetops and met her gaze. "It's crossed my mind once or twice. I know it'd get me ahead, but it doesn't mean I wouldn't end up in the same position later on, and then I wouldn't have them at all."

"Tell me the story," Callie pleaded. "You said that your grandmother gave them to your mother or something."

They came upon a steep incline in the path with a large boulder at the top. Callie panted up the hill and dropped Mark's hand to climb up onto the rock and sit down. There was a nice view through the trees.

He came up and joined her. Sun filtered through the trees, and she rolled up her pant legs to her knees. "Black pants get hot pretty quick in the summer."

"I bet." His chinos were ruined with smudges of wood stain. "You may have to start wearing shorts soon. It's going to get hotter."

"I love the Fourth of July, though. It's one of my favorite holidays."

"Mine, too," Mark said. "The parade marches right past the store as it goes around the square, remember, and business always does well."

"You work on the Fourth now?"

"Just in the mornings."

"I remember when you used to spend it with my family."

He smiled at her, and she realized how close they sat together. His light stubble had flecks of gold in it.

He smiled, and her favorite dimple appeared in his cheek. Her heart hopped, and she looked away, amazed that he could make her feel woozy.

"My great-great-great-grandmother passed them down through the family."

"The spoons?"

"Yes, Grandma Molly. Her father, John Friery, came from Ireland as an indentured servant to South Carolina as a boy. Once he earned his freedom, he worked on a few merchant ships out of Savannah for some years and eventually ended up with a small parcel of land somewhere near Atlanta."

Mark's smooth voice drew Callie into the story. She gazed off at the distant tree line across the lake where the water met land. Some of the tall trees around them, she thought, were probably standing at that very time.

"Molly was the oldest daughter, so I imagine she had a lot of responsibility and expectations. People did the best they could to marry well, and I guess that's what her father had in store for her but then the war came."

"The Civil War."

Mark nodded. "I can't even imagine what

they went through. Her father joined up and was wounded. Her older brother and two younger brothers fought, and all but the youngest died. Her mother became sick during that time and died, too."

Stories about war, especially slavery and the Civil War, made Callie feel almost ill. It was all so confusing—and there were so many regrets. She struggled with people who wouldn't admit it was a horrible, backward time.

"Anyway," Mark said after a pause, "when Sherman came through, Molly found herself helping a wounded man who'd hidden out back behind their house. Turns out, he was a Union soldier, starved, shot through the shoulder and near dead. Long story short, she nursed him back to health and kept him hidden from her father recovering in another part of the house. They fell in love with each other."

Mark seemed to be waiting for some kind of reaction, so she whispered, "Don't stop now. Tell me it all worked out."

He gave a faint smile, and she realized how much she always adored the color of his gray-blue eyes.

"Her father eventually caught them. Bailey Hart—that was the soldier's name—stayed on and helped with the house and animals until the war ended shortly after. They told everyone that he was a deserter to keep him from getting killed, but as soon as the carpetbaggers and scavengers took over the city, people had other things to worry about."

"Did they get married?"

Mark gave her a teasing grin. "It turns out he was the son of a wealthy politician from Rhode Island. When Molly's father put his foot down and said that there wouldn't be a wedding, Bailey Hart went back home."

"No!" Callie almost started to cry. "That's terrible! Why would you tell me that?"

Mark chuckled. "Well, because they wrote letters and when things became critical during the Reconstruction to the point Molly's family was literally starving, a case of silver spoons, forks and knives arrived for Molly."

"I knew it," Callie said as tears filled her eyes. "He sent her the spoons."

"Yes, with a letter asking her to elope. She was able to use the silver to get credit, and just before her father died, he changed his mind and gave his blessing for them to wed."

Callie gasped.

"But," Mark said, raising a finger, "it didn't make any difference. Bailey Hart had already settled his affairs up North. He was trying to convince his family he wasn't insane moving to the South. He arrived just in time to shake her father's hand and receive his blessing before he passed away. Bailey and Molly married sometime in 1867."

Mark finished his story and sat back. They gazed across the lake until a flock of small, dark birds swooped past them in a busy cluster.

"So," Callie said, dropping her legs and resting her hand over his on the rock, "they lived happily-ever-after in Atlanta and passed down the spoons."

Mark nodded. "Yes, to my mother and now me. She wanted Hadley to have them."

"I see why you want to save them."

"Bailey Hart could have forgotten all about my great-great-great-grandmother. He gave up his inheritance and a great deal of prestige leaving Rhode Island, but he'd fallen in love with a Southern belle, despite the horrors of the war."

"Did they consider him a traitor?"

"No. At least I don't. He never apologized for fighting for the Union. Saying he was a deserter before the war ended was Molly's idea, but you do what you have to do. It didn't just save his life, it likely saved hers and her father's, too. He probably changed his story and just explained the truth. Who knows what he did to protect them? That's why the spoons mean so much to me. He was a good man, he stood up for what he believed in and he stayed loyal to the very end, even to Molly."

Callie's throat knotted like a pretzel. She pointed at her tear-filled eyes. "Look what you're doing to me," she croaked.

He chuckled. "Do you see why I can't sell them now? They're probably the last thing he received from his own family. They were his promise to another a thousand miles away, and he kept it."

Suddenly, Callie realized she would never feel right about trying to talk Mark out of his spoons. Once upon a time, she'd tried to convince him to take a baseball scholarship. She'd tried to talk him out of his dream to join the Coast Guard instead of doing what he wanted to do at the time. She was glad she'd failed.

"Then don't do it. There has to be another way. Maybe I can help you with some updates on the store."

"You'd do that for me?" he asked.

"Of course I would." She realized it wasn't because he'd helped her fix the floors. She just would, no strings attached. He'd never expected anything back from her since she'd seen him again. He'd never been that way.

Callie realized they were simply looking at each other, and she felt a blush bloom across her cheeks. She gave a quiet, little laugh and watched his eyes crinkle around the corners. As if reading her mind, he leaned over and brushed his lips across hers in slow motion. When she opened her eyes, they moved apart, and he looked back out over the lake.

Callie was speechless. He'd never kissed her like that before. No one had. She stared out over the water, with him, afraid to even say a word.

Feelings she thought she'd moved past and erased had only been hidden, not fully healed. She'd been fighting them since she'd walked into the Market this summer to find him as handsome and sincere as he'd ever been; and more mature and thoughtful. Could this really be happening? Mark Chatham was making her fall in love with him all over again. And this time it was faster and harder.

But what if he broke her heart again? There'd be no city far enough away to get over him this time.

Chapter Nine

Callie decided to stay home the next day and work on her laptop. There were sketches to do and emails to write, although she couldn't send any unless she used her phone's Wi-Fi as a hot spot. It made for clumsy and time-consuming work, but she wasn't up to leaving the house for Wi-Fi anywhere else. With her planner in her lap, she slept off and on in short naps to catch up on sleep.

"Finally!" Amanda cried when she picked up the phone.

"I've been busy," Callie said in a cool voice.

"Mr. Martin is on a rampage! One of the house closings fell through yesterday because of a bad appraisal, and he just lost the bid to buy the Quik Mart on the corner of Broad."

Callie slumped into the couch and put her ankles up on the Queen Anne-style coffee table. "I texted you that things were under control."

"One text? I told you the farmhouse had flooded, and you ran off without telling me what you were doing."

"I handled it," Callie retorted. "By the way," she said, unable to fight off the warning to let things go, "thanks a lot for telling Mr. Martin about the floor without calling me first."

There was a pause on the other end of the phone. "What do you mean? I texted you."

"Yeah, *after* the fact."

"No," Amanda denied. "The real estate agent from Burlington called me after his showing and then I left a message for you at the office because I was on my way out. I did text you, just not right away."

"Well, the secretary was so happy to let Mr. Martin know."

"He must have called the other agent to find out what happened."

"It's fine," Callie relented. "Although next time I don't do something perfect, you could speak with me first."

"Callie," Amanda said in exasperation, "no one expects you to be perfect. I walked through a mud puddle once and tracked it all over the white carpet of a house I was showing. I had to pay for the whole place to be professionally shampooed."

Callie wrinkled her lip. "Gross."

"Did you get it taken care of? I haven't had a chance to get out there."

"Yes," Callie said. "Leave the listing up. Mark and I stayed up all night replacing the wet flooring. You can't even tell now, and I'll seal it in a couple of days."

"How bad was it?"

"Several floorboards around the window were damaged. I've moved the dining table out a couple feet to let it cure. It's just going to have to sit that way for a couple weeks."

"Sure, yeah, that's fine." Amanda sounded relieved. "By the way, Mr. Martin said something to me about you getting your real estate license?"

Callie frowned. "Why would he think I'd do that?"

"No, I mean he suggested it." Amanda hesitated. "I mean, I think so. It's not a bad idea. It'd be great if you were to stay in Ragland. You're already on staff and just doing the staging."

Callie narrowed her eyes. "What do you mean *just*? It's a full-time job. All I do is run around for the company like a stagehand. I haven't had any time to purchase inventory for myself to set aside."

"I know, and you're doing a great job! Everybody loves you. There's an offer on the Maple Street ranch house already. Did you know?"

"I needed to hear that. Thanks, but no, I don't want to get my real estate license. That's not in the plan. Either I start up a boutique by autumn or I head back to Nashville."

"Have you thought about consigning furniture with Mark on the side? You can do some high-end stuff, and it'd bring a whole new kind of client into his shop, not just collectors."

"That's an idea," Callie admitted, "but I still want my own place." She didn't tell Amanda that it'd already flitted through her mind. There were so many possibilities living just blocks from a respected antiques store, and she knew the owner.

"Listen, we're having a picnic out at the lake for the Fourth of July," Amanda said. "Everybody's going to be there. Do you want to come?"

Callie hadn't thought that far ahead. Mark's description of watching the parade and other festivities from his shop on the Fourth sounded like a fun way to spend the day. "I'll let you know," she said, afraid to commit.

"How about tomorrow night?"

"For a picnic, or do you need a babysitter?"

Amanda laughed. "Um…both. Todd has a softball game, and I could use some help with the kids at the field. They get so cranky after school."

A ball game meant seeing Mark. "All right, but dinner's on you," Callie said.

Amanda sighed with relief. "Meet me there at seven thirty, and I'll buy you a hot dog with the works."

They hung up, and Callie let out a breath. She'd been afraid of a big fight, another argument that would separate her from her sister the way disagreements and disappointments had separated her from her mother. The farmhouse fiasco had been fixed. She couldn't make any more mistakes if she wanted to keep working for Martin Realty this summer.

She thought about her father and realized she hadn't talked to him since she dropped by when she first arrived in town. They didn't speak often, but she knew he wanted to keep in touch. She flipped through the phone for his number and hit Call. He'd love to hear about her job on the wood floors.

Mark pulled up alongside his mailbox and pulled out the mail. A bill from his car insurance read Second Notice. He sighed in frustration. He'd never been behind like this. Speeding down the drive, he parked at an angle in front of the house and urged Hadley to hurry in.

"I'm hungry, Daddy."

"Give Daddy a few minutes, then I'll make us dinner."

She skipped toward the television, and he winced. There were leftover frozen meals he'd boxed up on a whim a while back, and now he was glad he'd done it. He'd teased himself at the time; he was becoming quite the homemaker.

Thinking about being alone still made him think of Callie. He couldn't believe she'd let him kiss her. It'd felt so natural, and she'd had a twinkle in her eye and a flush on her cheeks afterward. He was sure she'd felt something. She'd held his hand the whole way back to the car, talking and laughing, and that made him realize that he wanted this again. With her.

Mark picked up a browning apple from the wire fruit basket on the counter and munched on it while the microwave defrosted some leftover spaghetti. Callie still lived her life a hundred miles an hour, but she was solid, had a natural cheery attitude and was always sincere. He never had to guess what she was thinking or what she wanted. She spoke her mind and did it with a smile on her face.

The microwave pinged, and he reset it to a lower heating temperature. They sure still had a lot in common. They both appreciated the value and stories of the past, and she knew her antique furniture, even if she had no use for sports cards. Plus, they both loved being outside or on the water.

The doorbell rang, and when he opened the front door, he found a sweaty, short man with thinning hair on the porch. By the look of his dress clothes, he hadn't planned on spending the day outside.

"Hello," he said with a flashy grin.

Mark immediately knew he was selling something. He forced politeness. "What can I do for you?" he asked, as Hadley wandered over, grabbed Mark's hip and hung from his leg.

The man held out his hand to shake, and Mark accepted. "I'm Ronald Brown from Burlington Realty."

Mark froze. He put his hands on his waist where Hadley dangled. He was interested, but for all the wrong reasons for poor Ronald Brown. "What do you want?"

Brown wiped his hands off like he had sand on them. "Well, I was having a look at that lot across the street. How far does the land go?"

Mark's blood pressure kicked up a notch. "I don't know what you're looking at, but I own three acres across the way, and the rest belongs to the farm over on Taylor highway."

"Ah, I see," Brown said, like he didn't have

access to maps or satellites. "You just have a small patch of land there."

"Yes," Mark said, trying to be patient. "We used to own much more, but it was sold off years ago."

"And that old house down the way?" Brown continued.

"On my side?"

Brown nodded.

"That's my old family home my grandparents built, but it was sold around the same time. My parents built this place." Mark decided to act ignorant. "What're you looking at land out here for? Not much for sale."

"Oh, well," Brown said, "the farm off Taylor that comes up behind your lot across the street is going up for sale. They have over a hundred acres."

Mark raised his brows. He knew the place. He didn't know the farm was selling, though.

"So, it'd be nice to pick up the few acres you have right here. It's sitting right in the middle of their back property."

"Hmm." Mark hesitated.

"Daddy, I'm hungry."

Mark peeled Hadley from his leg. "Go into my room and get the treat jar off my dresser. You can have one piece of candy."

She looked at Mark in shock.

"Then watch your cartoon until Daddy's done talking and we'll go get a hamburger at your favorite place."

Hadley dashed off for her candy. Mark turned back to Brown, his mind racing. McIntyre had hinted that the bank wanted more land out this way, but he didn't know it was that serious.

"Well, I sold off some there to the south a while back," he said to the Realtor, motioning behind the trees lining the far side of the driveway. "I figured they'd subdivide it into big lots and put in a house or two, but it's still sitting empty."

Brown gave him a mischievous smirk. "Right, well, they're looking at more than a house on a couple of acres here and there."

An alarm went off in Mark's head. He forced himself to rest his hand on the door frame and act casual. "What do you think they want to do with all this land out here?"

"You've heard of Whiteside Developers?"

"Sounds familiar."

"Yes, they're based out of south Atlanta, but they have an office over in Burlington now. They're the ones that put up that development on the north side of Ragland. You know, a few miles down from the new superstore?"

Mark's throat turned dry so suddenly it hurt.

"You mean that fancy subdivision with the lots that are so small?"

Brown went from sweaty to gleaming. "Yes, I've sold three houses in there. Beautiful homes. Great lawns, quality craftsmanship and up-scale amenities." He leaned forward and said in a silky tone, "They even have a neighbor-hood pool."

Mark shifted around and tried to push down the swelling ball of nausea that had expanded in his gut.

"What do you think?" Brown had cooled off in the porch shade. Mark should have asked him in, but he'd been so shocked it hadn't crossed his mind. He stepped outside and pulled the door shut behind him. He motioned toward two rock-ing chairs a few feet away, and they sat down.

Brown looked so pleased about how things were going, Mark almost felt bad that he had to disappoint him. His heart thumped in his chest, but he tried not to show it in his voice. The hair on the back of his neck stood up. It was his very worst nightmare; his parents' fears, and Mc-Intyre and his banking cronies were all in on it.

They rocked for a moment, neither man speaking. Brown's motion was short and jerky, like he couldn't contain his excitement for a po-tential sale.

"I've been asked about selling." Mark motioned across the street with his chin but didn't mention the bank. "I only sold the acreage a few years back because it was too much for me to keep up, and my parents had talked about it once."

Brown nodded in sympathy. He probably wasn't that bad of a guy.

Mark relaxed his shoulders, which had pulled back tight. "I guess it looks trivial to keep the land across the street, but I like having a view and want to protect it. We used to have horses over there when I was a boy."

"Oh, yeah?" Brown smiled. "My daughter takes equestrian riding lessons."

Mark nodded. "We never did that, but this isn't really a farm anymore. I do have the hay cut and rolled every year."

"Nice little income."

"As long as they cut it, it keeps it down for me, and they give me a quarter of the profit."

"Oh, that's a good deal." Brown's frantic rocking calmed, and he seemed to relax. The evening air cooled. The sun melted from gold to bronze.

"So, it's like this," Mark said. "I have no intention of selling any land right now. Maybe in about twenty years or so when I'm ready to retire, and that's a big maybe. I don't want any neighbors too close next door, and I certainly don't want any across the road."

Brown looked crestfallen, but he seemed to understand. "I can see how you feel that way, and I'd say the same thing, but if you saw the proposals I've seen, you'd probably change your mind."

Mark stopped rocking. "What do they think they're going to do?" He waited for a response, hoping the man didn't clam up.

Brown bobbed his head in time with the chair's rhythm. After a pause, he raised a hand and pointed across the driveway. "A cul-de-sac would back up here to the road, and then skipping over your lot, a back street would run about a block from the eighth mile marker and turn west. You'd basically have houses on all three sides of your land over there." He stopped and thought. "They'd probably leave trees, but you never know."

"Right," Mark said. If the farm across the street sold, his land would be smack in the middle of a subdivision. They'd take down any trees along the fence line in a minute. He'd seen it all too often.

After a few minutes' silence while Mark absorbed the information, Brown stood up. "Well, I didn't mean to bother you, Mr. Chatham." He stopped himself and explained the gaffe. "I just wanted to get out here before someone else in Burlington or Ragland got to you, especially the developer. It's easier for them to come in here waving their money around."

Mark tried to look amused, but he didn't feel it. "I don't need any money. I'm not selling any more land." He gave a sharp shake of his head.

"I understand. There's a lot of old families out here and not everyone is ready to give up the lifestyle." He sighed. "Our area is growing by leaps and bounds, though. People are anxious to get out of the city and find a nice neighborhood."

Mark stood up and offered his hand. "I get it. I don't have a problem with the suburbs. I know owning a lot of acreage isn't for everyone. I just don't want houses all around me, not to mention seeing a strip mall go up and before you know it…"

Brown shook his hand and gave him a light tap on the shoulder with his other one. "It's just part of the future. Progress, you know. Lakefront property is too expensive for the average Joe, and there's so much undeveloped land out this way with the lake nearby, it makes it prime real estate."

"Thanks for letting me know," Mark said, and he meant it. Now everything made sense.

"Sure." Brown handed him a business card.

"If you have any more questions, or if there's anything I can do for you, here's my number."

Mark thanked him, waved goodbye and watched the man walk down the driveway to his car on the street. A buzzing at his ear made him jump, and he swatted a mosquito. He frowned. This was just the beginning. The rest of the swarm was on the way.

Callie began painting the hutch as soon as she finished at the office Friday morning. Her mind drifted back and forth between her work and Mark's kiss, and even Hadley, too, whose limitless energy and creativity amused her. She wondered if she would see Mark and Hadley on the Fourth of July, and how soon the Pierce farmhouse might sell.

It had a showing scheduled for Sunday morning, and she wanted to get the hutch done before then. The paint would be dry enough Saturday night to replace all of the hardware, and the cabinet doors and upper drawers, too. She smiled to herself as the milky chalk paint glided on like thick pudding.

Her phone pinged, and she leaned over to where she'd set it on the floor. It was Amanda wanting to know if she was still coming to the softball game.

Grimacing at the paint drips on her fingers,

Callie held the brush out a few feet away and carefully hit buttons on the cell phone with a pinky finger. She'd be there in time, she promised. And not because Mark's going to be there, she fibbed.

The house remained silent. She felt so comfortable and at peace here. Who wouldn't treasure this place?

It was strange that Ragland hadn't changed much in reality, but to her it seemed so different. Kind of like Mark now.

She really enjoyed his company. He was laid-back, thoughtful and kind. True, he wasn't the most social guy, but she could tell he still enjoyed people. He was a listener, a watcher, but that didn't mean he wasn't a thinker. He was a smart man, he just didn't seem to feel the need to advertise it.

Speaking of advertising, Mark definitely needed to work on that with his shop. The man felt so guilty for disappointing everyone that he couldn't see running a store the way his parents had wasn't working. But she hoped he was coming around.

She stepped back and admired her paint job. It looked fantastic. She'd picked up some different hardware that Mark had set aside for her at his store—it was going to be perfect.

Her phone rang, and she jumped. Wiping her

hands off on a towel, she caught the phone on the last ring, expecting it to be Amanda.

"Yes?" she said with a silly, country drawl.

"Uh, Callie? It's Brett Martin."

Callie shut her eyes and grimaced. "Hi, Mr. Martin. How are you?"

"Fine, Callie. I just had lunch with the testing proctor. Do you know her?"

Callie frowned. "No. What test?"

"The real estate classes," he said in a brisk tone. "I mentioned them in my voice mails, remember?"

"Yes." Callie's heart sank. "You mentioned there'd be classes at the community center, but I'm afraid it isn't something I'm interested in."

"Ah…" Mr. Martin sounded confused. "I'm sorry, we must have a misunderstanding here. I meant for you to take them. We'll pay the tuition, and you agree to stay on at a two-year minimum with me here. How does that sound?"

Callie's heart thudded in her chest, and her ears felt like they were stuffed with cotton. "I didn't know you expected me to do that," she squeaked. "I thought you understood, Mr. Martin, that this was just for the summer and maybe into the early fall." She cleared her throat. "I mean, I thought it was an option, should I need the job if I don't go back to Nashville, but all

I'd planned to do was stage for a few months for you."

Her boss hesitated. "Well, that was the initial idea, I agree, but you might as well sell some of these homes you're staging."

He was dangling money in front of her, and it wasn't fair. She needed to pay off her debts. She wanted her own boutique, but the bank was stalling her every time she called about the empty shop on the corner. She just couldn't start working real estate full time and be tied to that for several years.

She took a deep breath. "I'm happy just preparing the listings to show, and I really enjoy updating furniture. You have a lot in storage. I can get that all done."

"I understand," Mr. Martin said in a patient tone, "but I really need an extra agent, and I think you have what it takes."

Callie tried to decide if he was giving her an ultimatum.

"You seem to have a lot of downtime," he added.

"I spend a lot of time on the road," she said defensively, "like Amanda, but I'm doing a different job. The job that you hired me for, right?"

A long silence filled the connection between them with tension. Finally, he said, "That's our number one priority, yes, but I'd like you to have a license if you're going to work for us so you can fill in when needed."

Callie's shoulders sank. Then she squeezed the phone in her hand. "I'll check into that."

"Sounds good," he said, then said goodbye and hung up.

She hit the disconnect button. "I don't want to go to real estate school," she grumbled loudly.

Her voice echoed around the house. Pouting, she slumped down into one of the dining chairs. But did she really want to go back to her old job?

Selling houses would mean less time working on furniture projects. Being forced onto a career path was going to sidetrack her from her goals. She'd been hired on to stage homes, but they demanded so much help from her with other things, she'd hardly had time to go to flea markets or auctions, much less find an affordable space for the boutique.

Callie let the cell phone fall from her fingers and clatter on the floor. It wasn't like Mark cared whether or not she went back. He was wonderful, but he hadn't asked her if she'd thought about staying. She closed her eyes.

Why did life never go according to plan?

Chapter Ten

"Oh, Callie, it's not that bad!" Amanda marched beside her from the parking lot where they'd met toward the long line at the concession stands. She dragged Nicole along like an old blanket. The little girl whined for candy the whole way.

Callie tugged her white ball cap down over her forehead and reached for Justin. He was still a hand-holder; kindergarten hadn't changed that. She looked down at him, and he gazed back up at her with big brown eyes. "I love you," she told him, and he beamed up at her.

"It *is* bad," Callie said, turning back to her sister. "I don't want to spend my weeknights taking classes to do something I'm not even interested in. How long before I'm filling in to show houses for people that call in sick? I didn't take this job to become a real estate agent."

Amanda huffed. "Is this because I asked you to unlock the house on Griffin Avenue before you drove out to the farmhouse this morning?"

"No," Callie pouted. "Maybe."

"I want my grape lollipop," Nicole bellowed.

"Just wait a minute," Amanda snapped.

Callie laughed. "You spoil them."

"I do not. She's just greedy like her daddy." The line to the concession stand moved a few steps. "Five more minutes," Amanda promised Nicole.

"Haven't you fed them dinner yet?"

"No," her sister said with impatience. "That's what this is for."

Nicole screamed again. Callie looked away.

"What? Do you think you can do better? Wait until you're in my shoes before you start giving parenting advice."

"I know, I know," Callie said. She pulled Justin closer and wrapped her arm around him, and he hugged her leg. "I just wouldn't feed my kids candy for dinner."

"Ha! You just wait." Amanda dropped Nicole's hand and let her flop around on the ground.

"Well, I told Mr. Martin I'd think about it," Callie said. "But he pretty much told me I don't have a choice."

"I'm sorry." Amanda reached over and

touched Callie on the arm. "He never said anything to me about this before now. I guess he's trying to kill two birds with one stone and wants to convince you to stay."

"Yeah, well…" The whole situation made Callie angry.

"It's going to be okay," Amanda said. She finally seemed to get how upset Callie felt.

She swallowed, and the tears she'd been fighting back welled up in her eyes. "I just want to have somewhere to show and sell my stuff," she said. They moved up in line. Almost there.

"Well, at least you're back home. That was always Mom's dream for you."

"For now." Callie laughed, and the mood lifted. "And her dream was for me to marry Jeff Crowder and join the DAR."

Amanda laughed, too, held up two fingers to the woman working the counter and called out, "Two hot dogs with the works!"

Justin tugged on Callie's elbow. "I want gummy bears," he said in a polite whisper.

Callie looked down into his beautiful face, and the agony of the day disappeared. "Okay, sweetie," she said, reaching down to pick him up although he was a bit too big to carry around anymore. "You can have whatever you want."

When they reached the bleachers, Callie scanned the field until she spotted Mark throwing hard passes back and forth with one of the other players. He didn't have his ball cap on; his hair looked as golden as his smile while he talked to his teammate.

"Callie!"

She looked down and saw Hadley on the ground beside the bleachers digging a hole with a plastic spoon. "What are you doing?" Callie laughed.

"Come see my tunnel."

Grabbing Justin by the hand, Callie helped him to the ground and over to Hadley's project. They crouched over the meager hole.

"This is my dog house," Hadley announced, "but I have a cat."

"You do?" Callie raised a brow at her.

"I'm going to get one."

"I have a dog," Justin said. He studied the hole and looked with interest at the spoon.

"Justin, why don't you help Hadley dig a tunnel for the dogs and cats?"

They both seemed to think this was a great idea. Callie pulled a metal nail file from her purse and handed it to her nephew. "Don't poke anyone."

The kids went straight to work, and Callie sat on the bottom bleacher nearby, wondering why Lois wasn't there. It was nice that Mark felt comfortable enough to take Hadley along with him wherever he went, and people seemed to look out for her, but sooner or later she was going to need closer attention.

She glanced at the players on the field. Mark was looking her way or maybe at Hadley. He looked relieved when he saw her and raised his glove. She nodded. There was no way he could really concentrate on the game worrying about his daughter.

She watched him relax. Someone shouted from the dugout, and the team members jogged in to stand around their coach. Callie watched Todd high-five somebody, then say something to Mark.

She tried not to stare, but she couldn't help watching him. She noticed he acted less reserved when he played softball with his friends. Just like he acted the night he'd stayed up with her at the farmhouse laying the wood floor. He had a poker face when it came to business and acquaintanceships, but for his friends, he seemed to let the walls down.

Again she thought of the kiss he'd brushed across her lips. It'd been so gentle and tender yet at the same time sent her heart soaring into the clouds. A big smile broke out on her face. Just thinking about him made her happy, and more than ever, being with him made her feel like she was home.

* * *

Mark tossed his glove to the ground in the dugout with disgust. He glared out over the field at their opponents. He'd missed a fly ball that resulted in a run for the other team.

He looked back over his shoulder. Callie sat in the stands with her sister. Hadley still played in the dirt nearby. She hadn't run off. Lois had plans with her friends, so he'd dragged Hadley along with him to the ball field. The distraction must have affected his game, he decided, even though he worried less about Hadley with Callie nearby.

The Copperheads had caught up, but the other team managed an extra run before the third out. The loss stung.

Mark rushed to pick up his equipment before Hadley realized he was through and dashed out onto the field. The air had cooled. He glanced up to see if any stars shone through the ball field's bright lights, but he could only find the blue moon. Fireflies blinked on and off in the brush on the edges of the field. He hurried through the gate and headed for his daughter, anxious to say hello to Callie.

She was wiping dust off Todd's little boy when Mark caught up with her. "Hey, how's the house?"

She looked up and smiled as she climbed to

her feet. "Hi." The little boy stared up at him for a second, then pulled away and darted toward the field. Hadley ran after him. "The farmhouse?" Callie asked.

"Yes."

"It's great. They have two showings tomorrow and one on Sunday."

"That's good news."

"Yes. Amazing, really. In this market and at that price point, I'm surprised it's showing already, but it is a new listing."

"I'm sure it's because it looks like a model home."

"It's all in the camera angles," Callie said modestly.

"Don't sell yourself short. Are you all finished up?"

"I just have to move the hutch into the kitchen sometime tomorrow. Todd's supposed to come to help out."

"Oh, yeah? Is he going to be enough?"

"Sure, it's not that heavy."

"Okay then," he said, as if giving in. "Let me know if you need any help, and thanks for keeping an eye on Hadley."

"It was no problem." Callie bit her lip and held his gaze. "And thanks for the offer, but I know you have a store to run. Have any other Realtors come by?"

"A fellow came in yesterday from Taylorsville. I can't remember his name, though." Mark studied her and she returned his gaze, eyes beaming. "I really appreciate the referrals, Callie."

She nodded. "So, I was wondering… Amanda and Todd are having a picnic on the morning of the Fourth, and I need—"

"Gimme!"

They both looked over at Hadley, who was standing at home plate with the base in her grubby hands. Justin tried to take it from her and a tug-of-war ensued.

"Oh, boy." His concern that Justin might end up with a bald spot hurried him through the gate. "Put it down, Hadley," he said in a louder tone than he intended.

The kids continued to screech and pull the sandbag back and forth.

"Hadley."

"No." It was her favorite word since she could speak.

By the time Mark reached the pair, Justin was crying, and Hadley was using her legs like a ninja.

"Put the base down!" He jerked it from the kids, and they both burst into tears. Justin took off at a run. Todd, standing on the other side of the fence, grinned at Mark and waved him off as his little boy crashed into his knees.

Hadley pummeled Mark's thigh with her fists. "That's mine!"

"No, it's not," he stated.

She screamed in frustration, and he picked her up, tossed her over his free shoulder and marched from the field.

Callie still stood in the same spot, her brows raised.

"Welcome to my life," he retorted as he walked past her.

Hadley screamed again.

"Be nice, Hadley," Callie said, walking alongside them. "Daddy's tired, too."

Suddenly, Hadley quieted, and Mark let her slide down to the ground. He kept a firm hold on her hand, though.

"I've had a hard day," Hadley quipped through her tearstained face.

Callie knelt down beside her. "I'm sorry, honey. I promise it'll be better tomorrow if you go home, take a bath and climb into bed with your spoon." She passed over a wiped-off, cracked plastic spoon that looked like it belonged in the trash.

Hadley sniffled. "And I have to say my prayers."

"Yes, don't forget to say your prayers and pray tomorrow's a better day."

"And for a mommy."

Callie seemed to freeze, her attention focused on the little girl. Before the moment could be made worse, Mark bent down and picked up Hadley with one arm. "She has a long prayer list," was all he could think to say with an embarrassed chuckle.

"That's okay." Callie rose to her feet and forced a bright smile. "Good night. See you guys later!"

Mark barely got out, "Bye now," before she dashed over to Amanda and Todd, who were chatting with another set of parents. Children were everywhere. All of them looked innocent and angelic, Mark decided, except for the one in his arms.

He was halfway to the car when he saw another parent struggling with her child. Darla Perez had three boys swarming around her minivan, and two of them were throwing punches.

"I'm going to count to three…" she warned.

"Hi, Darla," he said with a tired grin.

She turned and put her hands on her hips. "Oh, Goldie. I'm about to lose my mind."

He motioned toward Hadley, still pouting in his arms. "I totally understand. How's the salon going?"

"We're okay. Expanding is looking good."

Mark remembered the empty store space

where the dry cleaner had been. Callie had mentioned it, too. "Did you get the space for the spa?"

She nodded happily, and he tried not to show his disappointment. "Yes, it looks like it's going to go through. We're excited."

"That's great, Darla. I'm happy for you all."

"Thanks. I'm so relieved the bank was willing to work with us. Matt McIntyre is a stand-up guy."

"Is he?" Mark wouldn't publicly disagree, but he wasn't going to sing any praises.

Darla kept chattering as the kids hopped in and out of the van. Hadley pulled on his hand, eager to join them, and Mark let her down. "He actually lowered the rent on the salon a little bit," Darla was saying, "so we could afford to pay rent on two places. It's going to be tight at first, but I think this could really take off."

Her news tasted like sour grapes on Mark's tongue. So the bank would come down a little if someone was willing to set up two businesses? It wasn't enough to be angry about, but it irritated him all the same. The new spa space had sat empty for a while and was an eyesore on the town square. He wished he'd thought about it for Callie before, but he wasn't sure about her plans. Did she still want to go back to Nashville? Or stay here in Ragland?

"That's good news, Darla," he repeated.

"Thank you." She seemed almost giddy. "We can't wait to get started, and hey," she said with a wink, "the type of people looking for a facial are the same people that will spend a little cash on some fancy furniture."

He smiled faintly. "An old junk shop isn't exactly upscale," he reminded her.

She swatted at him. "People will come. We've put in some cool modern stores around the square. Did you know they were thinking about shutting down the Grub 'n' Go and opening a sushi place?"

Mark looked at her in horror. "What? You're kidding."

She burst into laughter. "No, I'm dead serious. Ragland is on the rise, Goldie."

He nodded but realized besides the Grub 'n' Go, he was the only other not-so-new storefront. "Well," he mumbled, "let's just hope the rent doesn't go up."

"Think positive," Darla encouraged. She told him how much the bank was charging for the salon and spa space. It stopped Mark in his tracks. They stood at the edge of the parking lot in the near dark, ignoring the shouts of children, and he stared at her.

"What? I pay four hundred dollars a month

more," he said, unable to keep the incredulous tone out of his voice.

Darla's brows furrowed. "That doesn't sound right, but you are bigger. Y'all have more floor space, and you're dead center in the middle of the block."

He shook his head slowly and thought. "No, actually, I'm pretty sure your building has more square footage. It goes back farther."

"But you have two floors."

"That's just attic space," Mark said. "I mean, my grandfather converted a small corner of it into a bathroom, but there's attic space up the whole block." He exhaled in a slow, shaky stream. Why would the bank charge more for his store's rent than everyone else?

"It looks bigger." Darla shrugged and shouted at her oldest to stop throwing shoes. "So, maybe there's been a mistake," she added. "You're probably right."

Mark's pulse was pounding, but he responded on automatic, even leaning over and catching Hadley as she ran by chasing Logan. "Good luck then, I better get this child off to bed."

"Me, too," Darla agreed. "Goodbye, Hadley. See you at school."

"No, you won't," called Hadley, and Mark shushed her. It came out a little too sharply, but he didn't mean it. All he could see was Matt McIntyre's face and dollar signs.

After giving Hadley her bath and putting her to bed, Mark sat in the dark on the couch. She'd prayed for a mother again. Every time she did that, he thought of Callie, and then the disaster of leaving her to go to Florida, marrying a girl he hardly knew and not straightening up until his parents passed and he was suddenly a father.

Darla's news about how much she paid for rent was right there, too. It'd shocked him.

He concentrated on the crickets and cicadas playing their staccato notes outside over the sound of his heavy breathing. Something inside him felt ready to snap. He couldn't believe that all of the stress and worry he'd had to deal with the past few months had been intentional and dishonest—and if not dishonest, at least dishonorable.

McIntyre's smirking face seemed to glow right in front of him like a holograph. The bank had sent him a letter in January about the raised rent; no one had told him about the increase to his face. He tightened his jaw. They'd raised his rent on the store. They wanted to buy his land because a developer was looking at properties in his area. It came to him like a lightning bolt. It wasn't hard to put two and two together.

It was as clear as glass. He wouldn't sell the

lot across the road, so they were trying to make things tight, to force him into another sale so he could make ends meet at the Market. They were betting he would give up more land before the Market—or both. The understanding felt like a fiery punch to the chest.

He could have managed all these years without selling anything off, but there was no reason to keep all the extra acreage. He didn't need it; he didn't farm it, and it really was for the benefit of someone who would do right by it.

Ragland was growing. The bank would be thrilled to see a new neighborhood with potential mortgages go in. Mark tried to be fair. It was progress. Things were changing. In many ways, they were getting better, but it didn't mean all of the old ways had to go.

He slammed his fist down onto the cushion next to him. Not the Antique Market. There was always room for the old with the new. That was what made life beautiful. Mark didn't want to lose the Market—or his home.

He suddenly couldn't see himself anywhere but in Ragland. Even if he could buy a second house in Florida, this was where he belonged, and he wanted to stay—for Hadley. For himself. Maybe even someday with a woman like Callie.

Chapter Eleven

Callie sat in her office Monday morning with the door shut to hide her misery. Her phone buzzed, but she left it in her purse. The calls for help from Realtors trying to persuade clients to paint over their purple walls could wait. She studied the email showing the time and location of the first real estate class her boss had signed her up for without even asking for her approval. Thursday was the Fourth of July, and she'd hoped to sleep in, then head over to the parade on the square before Amanda's picnic. If she was up all night on Wednesday, she'd be tired and probably cranky.

Callie sighed and flagged the email to look at again Wednesday morning. The weekend had felt dreary, too, except for seeing Mark and Hadley at church. Amanda made a remark that it was nice to see him there regularly again, but they'd only said hello in passing. Things had felt a little weird since the mention of Hadley's prayer list.

When Amanda had to remind her about their Sunday dinner tradition, Callie dragged herself over with little enthusiasm. She wasn't sick, she was just tired, and in a lot of ways. It felt like she'd hit the ground running the day she arrived in Ragland and hadn't slowed down. Now, she had to brace herself for another fight. She didn't want a real estate license. She didn't want a long-term job at Martin Realty. Her dream was still the boutique, but she'd made zero progress on that.

The computer chimed, and two more emails came in. One was a reminder about the autopay to her credit card. She grimaced. She'd be lucky if she could get the bank to lease her a cardboard box. A second denial came in for her adjusted offer on the empty storefront on the square.

Her phone buzzed again, and she groaned, threw up her hands and reached back for her purse to dig it out. She froze when she saw the text from Mark.

She stared at his name on the screen. It was too late to ask him to the picnic at Amanda's. It'd be awkward now since Hadley announced she was praying for a mommy. Mark clearly wasn't interested in that. Was she?

Realizing her hands were damp, Callie made herself click on his waiting message.

Can you talk?

Her stomach roiled. That wasn't a line every girl wanted to hear when she was in…love? And she'd heard it once before from him.

Uneasily, Callie typed in Yes and waited. A few seconds later, the phone in her hand rang, and she answered.

"Hey, Callie." Mark sounded like he was almost out of breath.

"Hi." She started typing on her computer like she was super busy. The notes were just a jumble of words and numbers for her to-do list.

"Are you busy this afternoon? I'm just closing up for lunch."

"Oh, I, ah…" She sat up straighter in her chair. "It's a little early, isn't it?"

"Yeah, well, I thought I'd run past the Pierce farmhouse and see the hutch, if you were free. Did you get it done?"

"Yes, and moved in. I meant to tell you about it on Saturday." She didn't mention she'd decided not to text him late that night. He had a child, and the little girl had made a public announcement that she wanted a mother.

"Did you get the hardware on?" he asked.

"Yes, Todd helped with that."

"Nice. Want to go have a look at the farmhouse and then get a milkshake?"

Callie glanced at her watch. "Sure. I can meet you up at the store."

"I'm already pulling into the depot parking lot in case you said it was okay."

She asked him to give her a minute and shut the computer down, then dashed out the door.

Mr. Martin stood in the office foyer with his hands on his hips, talking to his secretary. He nodded at her. "We have two showings tomorrow. You did a great job on the farmhouse. I think it's going to move fast."

Breathless, Callie thanked him. "I'm taking an early lunch, and then I have to meet Amanda out in Taylorsville at a new listing."

He waved as she hurried out the door. She was glad he hadn't mentioned the real estate license class; maybe she'd get some fast cash if the farmhouse sold quickly.

Mark was waiting in his green pickup truck. She opened the passenger door with gusto and jumped in. "Let's go. I'm starved."

He chuckled. His hair looked combed back, and he wore his usual denim Oxford shirt.

"I don't think I've eaten all weekend," Callie admitted.

"Same. I did drink one of those packaged cold smoothie drinks this morning, but it didn't go far."

"Ah, I see," she teased. "So you're going to ruin that with a burger and fries."

He glanced at her, then back to the road. "I'll skip the fries."

"You didn't eat yesterday?" She wondered if she sounded too motherly. "Amanda always has me over for dinner on Sunday nights, and it's usually pot roast. Pretty good stuff."

"Wow." He went quiet for a moment. "That sounds like what my mother would make." He paused again. "I miss that."

"Not the same as Grub 'n' Go?"

"Not quite," he agreed.

Callie wondered if she should mention Hadley's prayer. He glanced over at her, and she figured they might as well tackle the elephant in the room.

"So…" she said, trying to sound casual as she looked out the passenger window. "About the other day…"

"I guess you heard about McIntyre?"

Surprised at his response, she shook her head. "I found out the bank, Matt McIntyre really, is charging me more rent than any of the other stores on the block."

Callie looked at him with concern. "When did you hear this?"

"One of the other preschool moms at the softball field told me. She works in the salon."

Interesting. Maybe he hadn't even noticed Hadley's faux pas.

"She mentioned how much rent they were paying, and I put two and two together," Mark continued.

Callie sat back in her seat. Their eyes met, and she could see how upset he was. "What do you mean?"

"They've raised my rent to try to back me into a corner. The bank wants to buy my land across the street and sell it to a developer so they can put in a subdivision. I told him I wouldn't sell."

Callie felt her mouth drop open. "So are they trying to blackmail you?"

"No, not like that. I'm behind with the rent being so high. If he can get me indebted to him, he knows my only other resource is my land. I sold a lot of it off years ago, but I didn't have any intention of selling more."

"Oh, I see." Callie folded her arms. "What a snake. Can he do that? You should get a lawyer."

Mark shook his head. The truck slowed as

they approached the farmhouse, and Callie saw the giant for-sale sign in front.

"There's really nothing I can do. He can charge whatever he wants for the building. He owns it. His family has owned it for generations. My grandfather and my father both tried to buy it from them."

"But McIntyre doesn't want to sell. Ironic," Callie said.

"I'm going to have to confront him about this, but I'm not sure what I'm going to say."

"Just be direct. You can do it."

"You make it sound so easy."

"If he's in the wrong, you have a right to call him out."

Mark said nothing, evidently soaking in her advice, so Callie hopped out of the truck, and he followed her into the farmhouse. "You should see this hutch, Mark. It looks great. I'm really proud of it, even if it is plain white."

"Nothing wrong with that," he chided.

"You have no sense of adventure," she teased. "I wanted to paint it yellow and blue." He groaned, and she laughed as they walked through the house.

"This place looks fantastic," he said.

"Thanks. I think it's one of my favorite houses I've ever done. I love it out here. It's quiet, but it's not too far from town, and the lake is just up the road. I'm smitten with the place, to be honest."

He stood in front of the hutch.

Callie watched him examine it. She'd stacked the shelves with mismatched china she'd picked up at his shop.

"This looks great, Callie. I bet I could sell it for twice now what I sold it to you for."

"All it needed was some TLC and a coat of paint." She walked up beside him and to her surprise, he put a hand on her back.

"I think I made a big mistake letting Brett Martin hire you first."

She grew quiet. She loved the idea of going to work at the Antique Market every day. It made her heart soar. If he was serious…but no. She eyed him. "I would love to get a hold of some of the pieces in that shop of yours."

He grinned. "Something to think about?"

She forced herself to laugh but didn't hide the bitterness. "Buy me a milkshake, and we can talk. Let me tell you all about the real estate class I start taking Wednesday night."

With one last glance at the hutch, Mark grabbed her hand. He held it while they walked out of the house together. "Callie, if you don't want a real estate license, tell him you aren't going to do it."

She nodded, his encouragement calming and

empowering her. "You're right. He's not going to like it, but I'm going to have to stand my ground. Be honest with him." She realized she would. She'd put it off long enough.

They went back out to the truck and made it to Grub 'n' Go in time to beat the lunch crowd. Callie found the courage to ask Mark about watching the parade from his shop, and to her surprise, he agreed. She mentioned Amanda and Todd's picnic at noon, and he seemed excited to join them.

His good company and attention made her quit worrying about Hadley's prayers and the Wednesday night class, so she hoped he'd forgotten about his problems with the Market, too, by the second round of French fries.

Tuesday morning, Mark planned to make an official visit to McIntyre's office. He found him in the parking lot, standing beside his sleek, silver sports car, grumbling into his phone.

Mark hopped out of the truck and tried not to slam the door. Just seeing the man made his blood run hot.

"How's business, McIntyre?" he called.

McIntyre looked up in surprise, mumbled something into the phone, then put it in his pocket. "What's the matter with you? Can't you see I was on the phone?"

"I just found out how much my neighbors are paying for rent on the square." Mark watched McIntyre's eyes widen. "That's right. It seems like I'm the only one with the big price hike this year. Would you care to explain that to me? Do I have extra square footage that I don't know about?"

"It's not the square footage," McIntyre retorted, clearly unsettled about where the conversation was going.

"You're right, it's not. I don't even have the same square footage as the Grub 'n' Go or the salon, so what gives?" Mark stepped up close so they were eye to eye.

"I don't set the rates for your contract. Take it up with the board."

"You're the chair, so I'm taking it up with you," Mark retorted. He glared into McIntyre's eyes. His home was at stake. "Why's my rent gone up so much? You must want me to sell you some land pretty badly."

"It's just business," the banker said in a cold voice.

"Oh, I think it's much more than that." Mark pinned him with a hard look until McIntyre glanced away. "Would you like to talk about plans for the new development?"

"No, I would not," McIntyre snarled, but his

eyes shone with guilt. "I told you, it's just business."

"Let's make an appointment," Mark suggested. "I'd love to hear more." He spun on his heel. Behind him, he heard McIntyre head inside the bank.

This time, Mark did slam the truck's door. The confrontation had been fruitless. McIntyre hadn't admitted to anything.

Slowly, his heart resumed its normal pace, but he clenched his fists. He'd never sell his land. No matter what it came down to, he wouldn't give it up—or the store if he could help it.

Mark drove calmly out of the parking lot. The bank was one step ahead of him, but he knew how to play the game.

Driving back to the Market, he knew there was no way he would win a lawsuit in court. He could certainly let the whole town know what the banker was doing, though. McIntyre wouldn't take too kindly to everyone knowing he was ripping off the Chathams.

If that didn't work, well… Mark swallowed and glanced at the spoon rack hanging behind him on the wall. From what he had figured, he needed about five thousand dollars to get caught up to July, and he would hopefully be fine for August.

The idea he'd dropped on Callie at the farmhouse lingered in his mind. It wasn't a bad idea. He couldn't afford to pay her right now, but if Callie would come in and redo some of the pieces he had that wouldn't sell and help him clean the place up to make it look like a nice home store instead of a dusty old junk shop, he'd fit right in with the other businesses around the square. That is, if she didn't hightail it back to Nashville.

He did brisk business that morning, stayed through lunch and sold Jake Barton an old Victorian washstand in the middle of the afternoon. As he left, the front door rattled again, and Mark looked up with hope. It wasn't a customer, but one of the sheriff's deputies.

"How're you doing, Patrick? You come to share a doughnut?"

The short-haired deputy laughed and tried to look bored, but the apples of his cheeks flushed. "No, I'm not here to shoot the breeze." He glanced around the room, then back at Mark. "You got a minute, Chatham?" He looked serious.

Mark nodded, mild concern tingling in his chest. "Come on back," he said and motioned toward the office.

The two men walked back, and Mark dropped into the chair behind his desk and motioned for Pat to sit down across from him. The deputy wiped a sheen of sweat off his forehead and sat while folding an envelope in half in his hand.

"Hot outside?"

"Yeah, it's hot outside," Pat complained. "Have you been out there? It was seventy-eight degrees at nine this morning."

Mark forced a casual chuckle. "It's only going to get worse."

Pat sat back. They'd known each other since grade school. "I'm hoping it's going to cool down before Thursday, but they're saying it ain't going to do nothing till next week."

Mark crossed his legs and put an elbow on the desk. "Am I under arrest or what?" He smiled but bit the inside of his cheek.

Pat blew him off with a wave of the envelope. "Oh, no, you know how it is. McIntyre complains about everyone."

Mark looked at him in surprise. "Is this about this morning? We did have some words, but that was it."

"I'm sure that took great self-control." Pat shot him a knowing look, and Mark shrugged.

"I'm not going to lie. He's doing me wrong. What's he want?"

Pat waved him off again. "Oh, nothing. He's just trying to make you uncomfortable. Here." He held out the paper. "It's not a warrant or anything. I don't know what it is. He just asked me to hand this to you if we spoke today."

Mark leaned over the desk and took it. "I assume it's not a threatening letter since he handed it to you."

The deputy shrugged. "Open it and see. I'm happy to be a witness."

The envelope was official bank stationery so Mark assumed it was from McIntyre's personal desk. He picked up a tarnished silver letter opener from the desk and slit the envelope open. When he unfolded the paper inside, he wasn't surprised to see it was just a letter with the bank's letterhead stamped on the top, but the contents made his heart stop.

Pat cleared his throat, and Mark looked up. He felt the blood drain from his face and saw the concern on Pat's face. "What is it?"

"It's an eviction notice."

The deputy raised a brow. "Your house?"

"No, I own that. I have two weeks to be paid up in full on rent on this place with late fees, or he's taking me to court and shutting me down."

"Wow." Pat wiped his chin with a shoulder. "You behind?"

Mark nodded. "A few months."

"Yeah. He kind of told us that, but I thought it was just June or something."

"No, since spring," Mark admitted. "He

raised the rent on this place, and it's put me behind."

"I'm sorry about that. I get it, trust me."

Mark knew deputies didn't get paid that much, and that they put their lives on the line every day. "Thanks."

Pat heaved himself up, and Mark jumped up to shake hands with him. He let the letter slip to the floor. After the deputy left, he sat back down in the chair and stared through the doorway. There was an empty space on the far wall where the hutch had been. The hutch that had doubled in value after Callie got her hands on it.

He sighed and picked up the piece of paper off the floor. His shoe had left a dirty footprint on it. He read it again, then crumpled it up and threw it across the room. Curveball.

There was no way he could come up with that much cash, not unless he took out a loan. Unfortunately, there was no way a bank in Ragland would give him one. McIntyre had too much power.

Mark scratched his chin. He was out of sports memorabilia worth selling. He'd already given that up. He still had the spoons, but that wasn't going to happen. Maybe he could sell just one acre from the most northern end of the property, and that would cover it. It'd appease them for now, he hoped, but they weren't getting the lot across the street. Hadley had the right to grow up in the country just like he did.

He stretched back in the chair, hungry. He checked the time. Callie was probably with her sister out in Taylorsville or checking out a new listing with one of the other agents. Brett Martin kept her hopping. At this rate, she'd never have time to open her boutique. Then she'd give up and head back to Nashville.

It suddenly dawned on him that he didn't want that, but it seemed to be what she wanted. He'd let her go once, hadn't he? Did he have any right to stop her?

He hesitated, not wanting to bother her, but his gut told him that she wouldn't mind. He hit her name in his phone's contacts list, and she picked up with cheerful enthusiasm. The sound of her voice lifted the invisible weight off his shoulders.

He laid back in the chair and closed his eyes. With a hand over his forehead to push the oncoming headache back, he told her everything.

Chapter Twelve

Callie woke up Thursday morning, and the first thing she remembered was giving Mr. Martin the bad news yesterday. His face had turned white when she made it clear that she had no interest in working as an agent and that she would not be attending the training. Her phone rang, and she groaned.

"What'd you do, Callie?" Amanda's tired voice croaked through the phone.

"You heard already?"

"I heard last night. You left the office, and then I had to take Justin to T-ball practice, so I couldn't talk until now. I don't know if Mr. Martin's going to keep you on for the rest of the summer, Callie. He's pretty upset."

Callie pushed the bedcovers off her legs and put her feet onto the floor. "It doesn't matter at this point," she said in a dull voice. "That's not the kind of work I want to do. I told him so, and that's that."

"But it's a great opportunity. The company would have paid for your training. It's a whole new career."

"It's *not* the career that I want." Callie's voice cracked, and tears that had escaped last night welled back up in her eyes. "I was happy to stage homes, I told him so, and he pays fair. I said I could supply furniture and other pieces as needed, but being at the beck and call of an entire office just isn't for me."

"He must have thought you were crazy—and ungrateful."

A single, hot tear streamed down her cheek, and Callie stumbled into the bathroom and sat down on the side of the old porcelain tub. "He looked shocked for a minute, then he said that's what he always expected. But it's not fair. He never mentioned this part of his plan when he offered me the staging job."

"Maybe he was listening to the talk in town."

"What talk?"

"People see you with Mark, you know."

"So? That doesn't mean I have plans to stay."

"They're just assuming you do."

"Well, if there's no boutique, I'm not."

"You are so stubborn." Amanda sighed. "You do realize you'll probably have to pay Mr. Martin for the part of the class fees he won't get back."

Callie rubbed her eyes. "I won't. I never asked him to sign me up."

"Maybe you could have told him sooner."

"Why are you taking his side? You know I hate disappointing people, but it's not what I agreed to when I moved back here. I just needed something to pay off the debt and—"

"I know. You want to have your own shop, and now…" Amanda exhaled into the phone. "You're right. What are you going to do if he tells you that you can't stay on?"

"I don't know," Callie moaned.

"Well, don't worry. We'll work something out."

Callie ran her fingers through her tangled hair. "No, you've done enough for me. If he lets me go, I'll pick up something else. Maybe I'll go back to Nashville early or move in with Dad."

Amanda let out a jarring laugh. "You will *not* move back to Nashville. You're not leaving me here alone again."

Callie swallowed. She realized she wasn't sure if she even wanted to go back to Nashville. She didn't want to leave Amanda—or Mark— she admitted to herself. She liked it here. It felt like where she was meant to be. Besides, what if he asked her to stay?

"Hey, don't worry about it today. It's a holiday. Get dressed and meet us at the lake around lunchtime."

Callie stood and stretched. A parade and time at the lake—with Mark. It could still be a wonderful day.

Red, white and blue banners fluttered from the street lamps around the town square. Mark parked his truck around back and walked through the Antique Market with Hadley skipping at his side. She was beside herself with excitement over the parade. He was trying to appear just as happy.

Instead, his mind was on the bank. He'd looked over the most recent survey of his land the night before and decided on a parcel to offer them. It was that or the spoons. He knew McIntyre would be eager to deal with Mark directly.

The problem would be getting the bank to give him a fair price. If it came down to it, Mark could also sell the lot across the road, but it would be a last resort. There'd be almost no reason to keep living at the house like he'd planned on all these years, not if he wanted any peace and quiet. He might as well move Hadley into town.

With a sigh, he unlocked the front door and

left it open to catch a breeze. Early shoppers strolled by up and down the block.

He'd just sat down behind the counter, while Hadley climbed over furniture, when Callie came in.

"Hi." She waved, and he looked up and smiled at her.

"Callie!" Hadley darted across the room and jumped on her like an overexcited puppy. Callie picked her up and gave her a hug, her eyes meeting Mark's. He saw her cheeks flush.

"How'd it go with work?" he asked.

Her sunny expression fell flat, and she set Hadley down.

"Not good?"

She looked away and shook her head.

"What'd he say?"

"You mean Mr. Martin?"

"Yes, I mean Mr. Martin." Mark came around the counter to meet her, wanting to take her into his arms. Could he give her a hug? Would she let him?

Hadley climbed on top of a piano bench and swung her legs. "Come sit on my boat, Callie."

"In a minute, sweetheart." Callie turned back to Mark. "I told him I wouldn't be getting my license," she said, "and he told me he'd have to rethink having me onboard."

"I'm sorry. That's foolish of him. Look at what you've done already."

She put a hand on her hip and tried to look like she didn't care. "I know, right? What's he going to do without me?"

An elderly couple tiptoed in through the door and gave Mark a questioning look. He waved them inside. "Come on in, we're open," he called, and they appeared happy to look around. The parade didn't start for an hour, but people were starting to set up chairs and claim spots on the sidewalks around the square. A woman and toddler came in next.

Callie tried to shake off her mood. She set a hand on his arm and pushed him back toward the counter. "Go ahead. I'm going to look around and start rearranging this place for you if you don't mind. It'll be therapeutic for me, and I'm sure Hadley can help."

"No, have at it. All the suggestions you've made so far have been great. If you see anything you think needs to be moved, go for it."

She started in the back corner where he'd repaired the leak. With the local radio station playing and the crowds growing outside the shop, he hummed along at the counter, sold a very expensive set of collectible cookware and watched Callie from the corner of his eye. Hadley stayed on her heels.

Within only an hour, Callie cleared out a space for headboards and rails and moved all of them to the back wall of the store. She set up one of the nicer bed frames, calling to him that they'd need a mattress for a display, and then started pushing china cabinets and consoles from the middle of the floor to the wall where the bed frames had been.

She walked through the store, collecting similar pieces, and set up a light oak buffet with folded handmade table runners on one end. Three sets of glass goblets were artfully arranged on silver serving platters, and all of the heirloom wedding china was spread out by pattern.

It made sense. He found himself helping her when people stopped browsing to get ready for the parade. "I like this," he admitted.

Callie pointed over his shoulder. "Your grandfather clock drives me crazy. I think you should move it over to this side of the store. It's almost in the aisle."

"I want people to see it."

"They'd see it better if it was up against the wall." She pointed to the front where the bookshelves were. "It could go up there. Put the tall stuff against the walls and the low end tables on either side of them so you can see across the room."

"I guess you're right." The siren of an emergency vehicle rang out, and Mark checked his watch.

"Daddy, let's go!" Hadley rushed to the door, peering down the sidewalk.

"Wait for Daddy," Callie called out.

Mark didn't have to warn her not to run off. "We have about five minutes. Let's go out and catch the show."

Callie grinned at him with shining eyes, and he felt relieved she'd forgotten about all of her trouble with her job. He admired her. She saw the shop through an entirely different lens than him, and it was okay. It worked. They'd always worked well together.

He glanced at his daughter, who took Callie's hand instead of his. Could all three of them work together?

They walked outside after Mark closed the door behind them. His eyes glanced at the spoons, a focal point behind the counter. He took his keys out of his pocket and locked the door.

They walked into the throng to cheer the first parade entry marching down the street. The line of small floats and local high school bands snaked around the square and back down Main Street until it reached Broad Street.

Callie whispered a compliment at his attempt

to French braid Hadley's hair, then cheered beside him as he clapped and whistled. Lois found them and stood by Hadley whooping at the clowns on bikes. Callie spotted Amanda and Todd across the street and waved.

Mark caught Callie's hand and held it. They both laughed at each other trying to catch the candy thrown from the floats one-handed. He caught a couple of lollipops and handed them to Hadley, then Callie pleaded for her to share, crowing at her success when the little girl gave one up. She unwrapped it, popped it into her mouth and gave Mark a wink.

The weather was perfect. The music, too. It'd been so long since Mark had felt this happy. His daughter was there, his friends were in the crowd and the prettiest girl in Ragland stood right next to him again.

A marching band came thundering down Main and brass horns trumpeted out over the square. Mark looked over at Callie and squeezed her hand. She flashed him her electric smile. His heart did a backflip like he'd just seen her for the first time. He stared, his mind jumping forward and backward, trying to tell him something.

When she turned back around to watch the parade, he put his arm around her waist. He'd given up enough in his life. He wasn't going to let her go so easily this time.

"Okay, that's the funnest parade I've ever been to, and I've been to a lot."

"Funnest?" Mark teased, and Callie wondered if it was for her grammar or her giddiness. "I'm glad you approve. Nothing like a twenty-minute parade through the streets of Ragland."

She giggled. "Okay, it was kind of short, but with everyone hanging out before and after, and all the chalk on the streets and everybody throwing candy, it was better than Mardi Gras."

"Much less wild."

"Right, that's what I mean."

They sat side by side in the truck as Mark steered down the highway toward the lake. Hadley hummed to herself in the back seat. Callie felt like she was flying. Work didn't matter anymore. She could worry about her future employment with Martin Realty another time. Not today.

She'd almost felt light-headed when Mark put his arms around her during the parade. He cared about her and for all the right reasons. He was a gentleman—and always had been.

"Are you ready for your sister's picnic?" he asked. "Should I stop and get anything?"

Callie shook her head. "No, I offered several

times, but she insisted we come out after we locked up the shop for the day."

"I'm not used to going to things empty-handed, but if you say so."

They made it to the small picnic shelter by the lake's swimming area just a half hour after the parade. Hadley had fallen asleep, and Mark eased her out carefully and rested her on his shoulder.

"So what would you think about refinishing the floors in your store?" Callie walked beside him across the grass toward people milling around picnic tables.

Mark tugged his baseball cap over his head with his free hand. "It'd be a lot of work, moving everything out to get it done, but you're right. It needs help, and it'd spruce the place up."

"And then some."

He smiled, and she thought he'd grab her hand, but Todd yelled and waved a Frisbee in the air at him.

"Your buddy's calling," Callie laughed. "Do you want me take her?" Mark handed over Hadley, and Callie rearranged her in her arms. "I got you," she murmured, paying no mind to Mark's long look.

They separated, and Callie went in search of Amanda. She found her opening bags of potato chips, and sat down nearby with Hadley on her lap until she woke up.

"How was the parade?" Amanda asked.

"It was awesome. Didn't you enjoy it?"

"Not with this bunch. I was this close to putting leashes on them."

Callie laughed, and a roused Hadley climbed down from her knee.

Amanda pointed. "The kids are playing over there, Hadley." The little girl made a beeline for Justin.

Callie put her hands on her hips and examined the long picnic table filling up with food. "What can I do to help?"

They set up sandwiches and sodas while chatting about the parade. When Amanda asked how things were with Mark, Callie said simply, "They're good."

"So?"

Callie pressed her lips together, but she couldn't hold back a giggle.

Amanda smirked at her. "I knew it."

Callie punched her on the arm when she walked by with a bottled water, and it turned into a water fight until Hadley got involved with Nicole and Justin and they all started throwing handfuls of potato chips.

After Amanda rescued the food, Callie and Mark crowded with Todd and Amanda's friends around the table and ate lunch. They spent the rest of the afternoon throwing Frisbees and playing volleyball while the kids ate Popsicles and waded in the lake shallows.

There didn't seem to be anything Mark couldn't do, and he laughed at Callie's futile attempts to return a volleyball. "I didn't get it over the net once," she moaned as he walked with her to the water fountain.

"It's not a big deal. You're good at other things."

Callie rolled her eyes and took a long drink of tepid water. "I want to see what's new down here these days. They have a Frisbee golf course across the street." She pointed across the park but could already see the course was over-crowded.

"Let's go for a walk," Mark suggested.

Callie craned her neck for Hadley.

"She's okay. Amanda said she'd watch her if we wanted to go do something."

Callie felt her face flush. Her sister was encouraging things a little too much. There were things to talk about, she knew, if this was going to be something real—and lasting—between them this time. She looked toward the tree line past the grainy swimmers' beach and saw a walking path. "That must go around to the place we walked to last month," she mused, and Mark nodded.

He grabbed her hand, and her heart quickened.

"It does if you wanted to walk about a mile that way to the boat ramp. It's shadier than here, though." He motioned back toward Amanda's picnic area in the sun.

He looked hot, and Callie felt overheated, too. A light breeze rippled through the trees. "I'll take it, let's go."

"I'm sorry I didn't bring a swimsuit now," Mark admitted as they strolled into the trees. "I didn't bring life jackets, sunscreen, nothing."

Callie chuckled. "You've been distracted."

She meant the Market and the parade, but Mark whispered, "I'll say," and she blushed.

They walked hand in hand. The air smelled woodier, and old leaves and pine needles littered the ground. Large ferns sprouted up from wherever the earth stayed damp.

Callie could still see the road through the trees on one side. The lake was barely visible in the other direction. "They probably have camping around here somewhere still, don't they?"

Mark nodded and told her about summers camping out with his dad and later with the guys when they were in high school. Eventually, the walking trail broke out of the trees and ended beside a new playground. Across the flat lawn in the distance was a different picnic shelter. He led her by the hand to a wooden bench that overlooked the lake.

They took a seat, and Callie sighed with contentment. Even with the shouts of children and the buzz of the occasional Jet Ski roaring by, she felt like it'd been one of the most relaxing Fourth of Julys she'd had in a long time, and it'd only get better. "Fireworks will be going off soon," she said, although it was still a while before dark.

She felt him watching her and looked back into his gray-blue eyes. They crinkled when he smiled. "Fireworks," he repeated in a husky tone. Mark leaned close. "Happy Fourth," he said, and she felt her concerns evaporate.

"Happy Fourth," she whispered, and her eyes drifted shut. When their lips touched, she thought she'd never been happier.

Loud laughter made Callie start. She pulled back in surprise at little voices. "They're kissing!"

Mark grimaced and looked over his shoulder, and Callie followed his gaze. Three boys were standing several feet away, pointing and laughing. A woman in the distance crossed the grass toward them.

"Hi, Logan," Mark said in a flustered tone.

The boys giggled again. He glanced at Callie and motioned with his chin. "That's Logan in the red T-shirt. He goes to school with Hadley."

"Oh," Callie said, watching who she assumed to be their mother approach.

The short, dark-haired woman took Logan by the arm. She shook her head in apology. "Hi, Mark. I'm sorry. I didn't know my boys were bothering you."

"They're not," Mark reassured her.

Callie looked sideways at him and hoped he'd minded a little bit.

He stood up. "Darla, this is Callie, my—" He trailed off. Callie stood slowly, feeling her cheeks get hot again, for completely different reasons. He didn't say *my girlfriend*, and it was true, she wasn't.

"Hi, Callie. I'm Darla Perez."

Callie reached out to shake her hand, unsure of what else to say.

"You're new in town?"

"No." Callie gave her a faint smile. "I just moved back. I grew up here, but I'm just back for the summer. I'm heading to Nashville soon."

She sensed rather than saw Mark look at her in surprise.

"Well, it's nice to meet you." Darla looked back and forth between Callie and Mark and a knowing look crossed her face. "Sorry again about the boys."

"It's no problem," Mark assured her.

Darla corralled the rowdy bunch and gave a brisk wave. "Oh, Mark, did you hear? We open on Labor Day."

Mark smiled. "Congratulations, and good luck."

"Thanks!" Darla waved and dragged her brood back toward one of the distant picnic shelters.

He waved back, and Callie raised a hand, then sat down with a thudding heart. Mark took a hold of her fingers. "So you're going back to Nashville for sure?"

"I don't know what to do. The store space I was looking into fell through, I don't have any inventory yet and I certainly can't put down a couple months' rent."

Mark frowned. "What will moving to Nashville solve?"

"I have contacts there and could get a new job fast."

"So why don't you wait and see if some other location opens up? Darla runs the salon next door, and they needed that space for their spa."

Callie pulled back in surprise. "You mean she's the one that got the dry cleaner's space?"

Mark nodded.

"Did you know she was looking at it?"

He shrugged. "I mean, I guess. She mentioned it."

"But I told you I was checking into that." Callie's heart sank.

Mark looked sheepish. "I guess I didn't think to mention it. You were busy with the Pierce farmhouse and seemed to like working for Brett Martin."

Callie put her hands on her hips. "You knew that was only temporary."

Mark reached out to squeeze her hands, but she couldn't look at him. "Callie," he said in a low tone. "To be honest, I didn't really think you were that serious about staying here."

"Or maybe you unconsciously wanted me to go. Because you can't run away this time, but you know I can't stay if I don't have a business opportunity."

He looked surprised. "Is that all you care about?" His tone sounded quiet, but it felt like a stab to the heart.

Callie jerked away. "What do you mean? What am I supposed to care about? I have to make a living. You have the Market," she said through eyes brimmed with tears. "You have Hadley. I have…" She choked back a sob and said, "I have nothing."

Mark tried to take her in his arms again.

But she pushed him away. "You did what you wanted, Mark. You wanted to leave Ragland, and you did it. You left me, you did what you wanted to do and got what you wanted. I'm still where I was when I graduated night school." She began to cry as the truth spilled out. "It didn't work out. It's probably never going to, so yes, I'm going back to Nashville."

"You could change your dreams."

"What?" She couldn't believe her ears. Didn't he understand what she'd always wanted?

"You did do what you wanted, Callie."

Callie froze.

Mark threw her a terse look. "You wanted to move to Nashville. You earned your design degree. Can't that be enough?"

"It wasn't enough for you."

"Seriously?" Mark let out a sarcastic laugh. "I'm sorry I didn't move to Nashville with you. I really am. I'm sorry I didn't talk you into coming to Florida. I was confused about my future, about you, and I had to get away."

Callie blinked in surprise.

"Do you think I was really happy down there all by myself? And then Dad died and Mom got sick, and I couldn't come home. Not until I finished my coast guard service contract." He shook his head. "I fell into a relationship with Lisa because I was lonely, and it was a mistake. After we eloped, she completely changed her mind about being in a committed relationship and went back to the party scene. Pregnant with my baby."

Sympathy pierced through Callie's pain. His eyes looked wet, and it melted her heart.

"I've never been more sorry," he insisted. "I never forgot about you. Never!"

He stepped back and took a deep breath. A stiff breeze brushed past them, and Callie turned to look out across the lake. She'd made a mistake coming home. As much as she loved it, and seeing Amanda and the kids, it was just too painful. She'd never gotten over Mark, and he was everywhere here.

"I should have never moved back," she whispered. She felt him shift beside her but didn't look. "You're right, Mark. I should give up on my stupid boutique dream and just get back to work."

"Callie, I never said that." His tone sounded serious and demanding at the same time. She couldn't bear to rehash it all over again.

Callie wiped the tears streaming down her face and ran off for the footpath in the trees. What a disaster. She gritted her teeth to keep from sobbing.

What had she been thinking? That she could turn things around and have her own business in three or four months? Did she really think Mark would support her this time when he hadn't years ago? What did he want from her? A summer fling?

The sound of pounding footfalls came up to her, but Callie didn't slow down or look back. She winced when Mark swept up beside her. Panting lightly, he took her wrist and tried to slow her down.

"Callie, wait."

"Stop." She jerked away and kept walking. Mark hurried to catch back up and walk alongside her. Callie's leg muscles and hips screamed for her to stop. She'd get shin splints even if it killed her.

"It's not what you think," he said.

She shook her head. She hoped he'd trip over a tree root for not paying attention to where he was going.

"I didn't intentionally not tell you about the store space," he went on. "And yes, I did like the business you were sending me from the other Realtors, but it was something more."

Callie locked her jaw but kept moving.

"Please stop." Mark's voice sounded hoarse and upset. It was enough to slow her down.

Her heart ached to hear an explanation. Something. She slowed her walk, breathing hard and breaking out in a sweat.

"I wasn't trying to undermine you. I did want things to work out for you here—why wouldn't I have wanted you to stay? It's just—I wanted things to work with us, too. I wanted to try again. I just didn't know how to ask."

"Don't you realize me moving back to Nashville would have ruined that?" she asked in a biting tone.

He nodded. "Maybe I knew that in the back of my mind, but it was never intentional. I guess I was curious to see what you'd think of Hadley, and if…" he hesitated "…if you'd grown up."

Callie's resolve snapped. She came to an abrupt stop, and he skidded into her. She put her hands behind her back when she turned to face him so he wouldn't see her wringing them. "It would have been nice to know you thought I was too immature to handle a man with a child before you came to this picnic with me."

He held up his hands. "It's not like that…" He looked overhead, and she could imagine his mind racing. "She's a handful. I've never tried to have a long-term relationship with anyone since she's been born."

"You know what I mean," she said.

He stared, and his face seemed to lose color. "I care about your daughter."

"That's all I needed to know."

"Before what? Letting me move back to Nashville?" Her eyes watered.

Mark's face flushed. "I want to have a relationship with you again, Callie. I just needed to make sure you were ready. That I was…"

She choked back a sob. "We were never meant to be, Mark. You should have kept it business." She marched toward Amanda's picnic tables with his footsteps behind her.

A loud scream from the lakeshore grabbed her attention and then she heard Amanda cry, "Hadley!"

Callie's legs took off at a run.

She couldn't see Hadley, but she saw flailing arms in the water out by the safety buoys, and then Amanda leaped into the water from the shore.

Mark sped past Callie, and then she hit the lake at full velocity, a sloppy dive that morphed into clumsy strokes. Amanda had stopped shoulders-deep in the water, and Mark stroked past her like an Olympic swimmer.

Callie saw Hadley's arms sink down below the surface, and a shriek echoed in her ears. It was her own. She swam out to the buoys and reached Mark just as he came up with his sputtering, gagging daughter. Callie treaded water beside them, and she shouted for him to flip Hadley over. "She's still choking!"

He tossed Hadley over his shoulder and beat her on the back until she cried.

Callie sobbed right along with her.

The crowd on the shore circled around them after Mark reached the shore. He collapsed into the muddy sand and held his daughter while she cried and coughed. Callie put her hand on his shoulder and crouched beside him. She embraced Hadley, too, her eyes streaming with tears of gratitude.

"I'm okay, I'm okay, Daddy," Hadley chanted between sobs.

"You are okay," Callie reassured her. Hadley reached out a hand for her, and Callie grabbed it. "You're going to be fine, baby."

The little girl raised her head off of her daddy's shoulder. "I got in over my head," she sniffled.

"I know, honey," Callie whispered, patting her on the back over Mark's hand. Their fingers touched. She glanced down at the man she still loved. He was frozen in horror at the near accident.

Callie choked back another sob. "I got in over my head, too."

Chapter Thirteen

Mark sat beside Hadley while she slept until moonlight lit up the bedroom, and he knew it was near midnight. He'd taken her straight home without a word to Callie, who'd stood near the truck quietly sobbing. It was almost like the scene he'd experienced before—her crying and him leaving.

He swallowed bitterly and looked down at Hadley sleeping like an angel. Of course, he'd been the one to leave the first time, but now it was Callie. She could stay if she really wanted, if she loved him. Why didn't she tell him she was waiting for him to ask?

Hadley shifted in her sleep, and Mark put a hand on her back to feel her heartbeat. Lisa had died of a rare aneurysm during labor and delivery, but Hadley was in perfect health. But he'd nearly lost her today.

He slumped over from the weight of carrying his parenting load alone. Maybe Callie was right. Maybe he never really believed she'd stay in Ragland. Maybe he was too afraid to ask her, to beg her, like she had him once upon a time. He knew he wanted her to, though. He wanted lots of things, he admitted. He wanted her in their lives.

His eyes watered and spilled over as he recalled Hadley's bedtime prayer. She had sobbed through being sorry for not listening to Amanda. She'd prayed she could still have a cat. She'd thanked God she hadn't "drown-ded," and then she'd glanced up at Mark for a second before bowing her head and saying, "And can I still have a mommy like Callie?"

It tore at his heart that his daughter was in love with Callie Hargrove, too.

Mark leaned down and listened to make sure Hadley was breathing. Satisfied, he sat up. For the first time in what seemed like forever, he decided he needed to start praying again, too. He was too thankful to still have his daughter not to express his gratitude, and if he was honest, there were things he hoped for and needed.

Later that morning, he dropped Hadley off at Lois's house and drove past the Market to the bank. Today was the day. The clock on top of the courthouse said it was eight thirty. He was early, but he'd called Wednesday afternoon just before closing and left McIntyre a message to expect him.

Mark drove into the lot with his mind swirling over Callie's disappointment in him and saw McIntyre's sports car in the reserved parking spot. If he was ten years younger, he would have pulled in right behind it to block it in, but this wasn't child's play.

He took a deep breath and exhaled before he climbed out. He couldn't outdrive or even outdress the man, so he'd just put on his usual khakis and work shirt. At least he'd worn a belt. Balancing the jumble of papers in his arms, Mark walked to the front doors.

Two tellers stood at the counter chatting when he breezed in, and they both stopped talking at the same time. The bank opened at eight thirty, and he was the first customer of the day. One of them glanced sideways toward McIntyre's office.

Mark didn't walk all the way up to the counter, just said, "Hi, Miss Julie. Is the boss in?"

Both tellers nodded at the same time and Julie, a longtime friend of his parents, pointed. "He's waiting for you." She gave him a look that seemed to say *good luck*, and he pressed his lips together in a small smile. She probably knew what was going on, which meant the whole town did, too.

Mark knocked on the heavy door and waited for McIntyre's voice to call, "Come in." He sounded serious. Of course he would.

Mark strode in pretending like he was relaxed and not like his heart was thumping in heavy, jerky beats. McIntyre didn't stand up. Mark didn't wait to be invited to sit down. He held his gaze until he reached the chairs sitting on either side of the desk and dropped into one, then he crossed an ankle over his thigh like they were just going to have a casual conversation.

McIntyre spoke first. "You're early."

"I figured you'd be here."

The banker looked down at the keyboard in front of him and pushed it out of the way. He leaned back in his black, high-backed chair. "What'd you bring me?"

Mark didn't mention the final notice, not the one the deputy dropped off or the certified copy he had to sign for on his front porch. "Less than two weeks is not a lot of time to gather thousands of dollars together."

The man across the desk shrugged. "There's loans, credit cards, liquidations. I'm certain anyone of reasonable intelligence could find a way."

Mark ignored the IQ insult. He'd heard it a lot growing up as a jock.

"You know how I operate," Mark said. "I'm honest." He gave him a cold stare, then flipped open the leather bank book that had been his father's. "You've given me no choice, but I'm only selling an acre."

"That's all I need if it appraises for the right price."

Mark blinked. "Cut the act. I know you're in with the developers, and I know you want my land—all of it."

McIntyre looked surprised, but he smiled. "Then you understand it's just business. The real problem is you can't keep up the rent on the Antique Market. So we have two orders of business to discuss."

"No, just one." Mark cut him off. He tossed the survey map onto the wide desk. "You can have an acre on the north end. It runs from the barbed wire fence to the hayfield that sits next door to my house."

The banker picked up the piece of paper by the corner and glanced at it. "I'm actually interested in a little more than that."

Mark shook his head. "I'm not selling the land across the road. I don't want a subdivision in front of my house."

McIntyre made a noise that sounded like a strangled but amused chuckle. "You don't really have a choice, Chatham."

Mark inclined his head like the man made no sense. "I don't owe you anything but cash, McIntyre, and you want a piece of land, so take it. That's all I'm offering."

McIntyre pushed the survey back across the desk toward him. "That's not going to work for me. I don't have to buy anything, you understand." He lowered his head and looked at Mark almost through his eyebrows. "I won't buy any land from you unless it's all of it."

Mark sat motionless in the uncomfortable chair, his mind spinning.

"Let me tell you how it's going to be," McIntyre said. "You will sell me everything, the land, the house and the lot across the street, and I will forgive your default on the shop payments. Completely." He set his elbows on the desk and steepled his fingers. "I'll even reduce the Market's rent back to the amount you paid last year."

Mark's ears rang. It felt like hot lava roared through his skull. The room fell silent.

"Do you understand?"

Mark could hardly get the words out. "You want me to sell my family home so you can build yourself a flashy neighborhood?"

"If you want to keep the Antique Market open. You'll be well compensated for the land." McIntyre flicked his wrist like money was no object. "You'll be out of debt and then some.

Look, Chatham, you could pay cash for a brand-new house in the subdivision. You could have the first build."

Mark stood up, his mind racing. He had to get out of there before he jumped over the desk. "You must be out of your mind," he whispered in a low tone.

McIntyre had the good sense to look intimidated. He glanced toward the door like he was thinking about screaming for security. "It's all or nothing," he responded. "I don't want your measly acre, and you have ten days from now to come up with seven thousand dollars or you're out. You will never sell another decrepit old rocking chair in this town. We don't want the Market there anyway. You're slowing down progress with that dump."

Mark drew in a sharp breath. "You can't do this."

"I can and I will." McIntyre smiled like a snake. "There's no time to sell your land through other channels. This bank is not going to do business with you, and I'll make sure no one else does, either. Sell me the land, buy yourself a trailer on the other side of the county, and maybe, just maybe, I'll let you keep the store space."

Mark got up and started walking for the door. He needed to think. There had to be a way to get a cash advance from somewhere, somehow.

The only credit card company he hardly ever used had agreed to three thousand. He needed to come up with the rest.

He imagined the sound of evil cackling behind him as he stumbled out the bank doors into the bright sunshine. Squinting, he clutched the account book to his chest like a pillow. He should have just put the store space rent on a credit card and taken the hit on interest. Now what would he do? The only answer was…the spoons.

He slammed the door to the truck and sped out of the parking lot. It was all he could do not to mash the gas pedal. The truck bounced across the train tracks and turned into the depot parking lot. Callie's car was there.

Heart pounding, he pulled up beside it to sit a few minutes and try to calm down. Maybe she'd come out and talk to him. Maybe she'd forgive him for yesterday and hear him out. He glanced at her car.

To his surprise, she was sitting inside it with the windows rolled up. She looked over through the window, obviously shocked to see the truck idling beside her. Her face looked red and tearstained.

Callie couldn't believe it when Mark pulled up beside her. She wiped her face with her palms and sniffed. Somehow, he must have known. She'd been crushed, feeling sorry for herself, and like a beacon, he'd picked up on it and showed up. She watched him get out of the truck, his face filled with concern.

She didn't even argue when he came around to the passenger side and looked in with a questioning look. She gave a swift nod, and he opened the door and climbed in.

"Are you okay?"

She wiped her face again and nodded. The wadded-up tissue in her fist felt wet and gross.

"Callie," he whispered. He put a hand on her arm. "I am so sorry. If I would have known the store space on the square meant so much to you, I would have said something."

Her eyes spilled over with tears. "Everyone's taking your side," she squeaked, and forced a dry laugh and sniffled. It was true. Todd and Amanda had defended him after Callie told them everything. She'd spent the entire night tossing and turning.

"I promise you," he repeated in a quiet tone. "I want you here more than you could ever imagine."

Callie wanted to believe it was true. "How is Hadley?"

"She's fine. There doesn't seem to be any

harm done. She wasn't even coughing this morning."

"Did you make her go to preschool?"

"No. Lois is watching her. I had to go to the bank for an appointment, but I wanted to talk to you more."

She wanted to believe him. "I just don't know what to think," she said and swallowed again to keep from choking on another round of tears. "Every time I try to take a step forward—" she motioned toward the depot "—stuff happens."

He slid his hand down her arm and took her damp fingers in his. "I'll help you find a place. We'll figure something out."

He took her chin in his other hand and made her look at him. It melted her heart, but he didn't know yet. There were more things. More problems that she couldn't even deal with right now.

"I got let go."

His eyes widened. "You what?"

"Mr. Martin just told me to move my things out of my office for a new Realtor. I can only stay on part time." Her eyes flooded. The early-morning confrontation had been humiliating.

Callie wiped her cheeks. "It's just like always," she muttered. "I do the best I can, give it a hundred percent, and things still fall apart."

"Honey, that's just life. It's not your fault," he reassured her. "You had every right to stand up for yourself. You never agreed to get a real estate license here." He squeezed her hand. "I'm proud of you. You fight for what you deserve. Not many people do that."

It was true, but look where it had got her. Callie peered through the windshield at the giant window that had been her first office. "With the pay cut, I won't even be able to make rent on the cottage now. I'm back to square one." She stopped for a pause. "I've got to find something else to do." She sighed. "You were right. I should just give up on it forever."

Mark leaned back in the passenger seat. The cool air from a vent blew on his face, making short tendrils of hair flutter across his forehead. He looked tired. When he opened his eyes, he turned his head to look at her. "Don't you do that, because I'm going to have to sell the spoons."

"What?" Callie wasn't expecting that. He'd been so determined, so committed and so loyal to his family heirloom, she couldn't believe her ears. "Why?"

The sadness on his face grew deeper. "The bank won't take the acre I offered. They want it all."

She felt the air whoosh out of her chest. It made no sense. "Who would do such a thing?"

"That subdivision is going in whether I like

it or not, and I don't have the money to fight it," Mark explained.

"But why the spoons? What are you going to do?"

He sat up, and she felt childish for crying over a job when the man beside her could lose everything.

"I always knew it'd come down to the Antique Market or the land someday. And I know I really don't need to have it, not on paper, but it's my—"

"It's your home," she said in a quiet voice. "Your life. The house and the land, too. All of it. You enjoyed going to Florida and all that, but this is home."

Ragland was home. His home. And hers. Did she even care about living in Nashville anymore? Opening a boutique?

Life was so unfair. Callie tightened her fists. "You can't do it. You can't sell, and you can't give up the spoons. There has to be another way."

"That's what I thought, but it's the only answer." Mark sounded beaten. "I have to choose between land or silverware." He gave a forced chuckle. "My home and the Market, or a hundred-fifty-year-old set of flatware."

Callie felt sick for him. She loved the spoons, and she loved how much he loved them.

He sighed. "I know a guy in Atlanta who'll take the spoons in a heartbeat. He's a collector and auctioneer—has ties with auction houses in New York. He'll get me top dollar even if I have to ask for an advance for them."

Callie sat back in her seat. The morning sun hung higher in the sky now. It was still early, though. "Mark, I'm so sorry. I really am." She squeezed his hand. "I have a little. It's yours if you want it."

He shook his head. "I can't take money from you. You'll need it for your move back to Nashville...but I don't want you to go, Callie. I don't want to live here without you again."

Callie's heart leaped in her chest. His words meant everything. He wanted to stay, and he wanted her to stay, too. Deep down in her heart, she did want to stay. Home.

She put a hand on his. "You know what? I don't think I am going back to Nashville. I need a job, yes, but I'm sure I can find something else around here, even if it's the Grub 'n' Go."

Mark's mouth broke open in surprise. "Say you'll stay, Callie," he whispered. "Stay in Ragland. Here. With me."

Callie's throat knotted up and a little squeak escaped. Was he asking her to be with him for good? She nodded as fresh tears cascaded over her eyes, and leaned into him. He took her in his arms and kissed her. It was comforting and warm all at the same time. Her heart sang.

"I'll stay," she laughed hoarsely, pulling back. "What do I have to lose? Besides," she reminded him, "I promised Hadley I'd take her canoeing again sometime."

"I'm sure she hasn't forgotten. Can I come with you?"

Callie looked up at him. "Always."

He tried to smile, but it came out more a grimace. "Callie, would you come to the shop and help me pack up the spoons?"

She started to answer, but the earth began to rattle and shake. They sat back with clasped hands and watched a giant locomotive roll by, pulling a line of train cars behind it. The sound drowned out her answer, but she knew he knew.

It was a gloomy weekend for the Antique Market. Callie wrapped up the spoons for Mark while he went back to his office to make the phone call. When she finished packing the spoons, she started cleaning out the front of the store beneath the windows by going through the boxes and baskets of toys. She discarded some and saved others to suggest he sell online or donate.

Moving what she felt was worth keeping to the back wall for later, she started dusting and polishing the flooring as she moved chairs around. He had several nice ones, including a little gossip bench and its attached side table. The seat needed to be upholstered. She made a mental note to ask him about it, and when he came out glumly to the counter, she gave him a long hug and asked him to call her later.

She headed home at lunchtime, not sure of what she should be doing. Mr. Martin had said he'd call her when he needed her. She'd be paid on a per-project basis. She groaned under her breath as she pulled into the driveway of the cottage.

Amanda sat on the front porch in a skirt and heels. Her minivan was parked on the street, and Callie hadn't even noticed. She took a deep breath and climbed out of the car. Amanda stood up on the front steps before Callie even reached the porch.

"It's not right." Amanda shook her head and put her hands on her hips. "I'm so mad I could quit."

"Don't do that," Callie warned, "or neither one of us will have a job." They embraced, and Amanda gave her a tight squeeze. It was just what she needed.

"I'm sorry, sis. I feel like it's all my fault." Amanda's voice cracked.

"Don't cry," Callie laughed as her eyes filled

up with tears. "I'm going to be okay. I'm always okay, right?"

Amanda frowned. "So I guess you're going back to Nashville? I feel like I let you down. I wanted you back here so bad and got you into this."

Callie hugged her again, then looked around for her house key. "It's okay," she reassured her. "I'll figure something out. I always do. Meanwhile, I need to get my laptop and stuff set up in there and clean up."

"Let me help," Amanda insisted.

"You're supposed to be at work."

Callie walked into the house. There were boxes all over the living room with paintbrushes and knickknacks everywhere. She'd been too upset to do the dishes the night before. "You can wash the dishes," she called, "if you're going to stay."

"I am going to stay," Amanda declared. She didn't balk at being asked to wash dishes, either. "But you really need a dishwasher."

They cleaned the house up together, even scrubbing the bathroom and gathering the laundry. Callie told Amanda about how Mr. Martin delivered his bombshell when she walked into the office, and then she told her everything that Mark had told her about the bank.

She felt justified when Amanda acted appalled, too. "What is wrong with people?" she cried, shoving towels into the ancient washing machine. "Everybody's so greedy these days!"

"Poor Mark," Callie said with some bitterness. "He's worked so hard, but they've set him up to fail."

"All in the name of progress," Amanda finished. She walked into the living room and plopped onto the couch where Callie was folding bedsheets. "How are things between you? Okay? Did you talk about yesterday?"

Callie nodded. "He asked me to stay. In Ragland."

Amanda's jaw dropped. "You're not going back to Nashville?"

Callie grinned and shook her head. Her sister squealed, and they rolled across the couch laughing.

"Y'all are good then?" Amanda sat up, her mind a one-track locomotive.

Callie felt her cheeks flush and realized she was happy. Really happy. "We haven't talked about anything long-term, but yes, he asked me to stay. Pleaded, in fact."

"Knew it." Amanda sniffed. "He should have never left the first time, and it's time for you to come home now."

Callie hung around the house Monday, waiting for Mark to drop off Hadley. She had begged not to go to school while her daddy went out of town, so Callie insisted that she keep the little girl while Mark drove to Atlanta to sell the spoons.

Packing up his spoons had been heartbreaking. She thought about how sad it would be if the story of the spoons became lost forever. It was really important, she told Mark in their late-night phone call, that he write the story down.

When he finally arrived, she sent a curious Hadley around the house on a scavenger hunt that she'd set up with treats, then spoke to Mark in the kitchen. He'd been resolved, and her heart ached for him, but she promised him Hadley was in good hands. They'd play games and eat snacks, she promised.

He thanked her again and kissed her softly on the mouth, but it was too brief, because Hadley came bounding down the hall with a question. She stopped short and stared at her father, and he'd told her a joke and quickly left the house.

Callie puttered around the house, spotless now thanks to Amanda, and played with Hadley until she fell asleep on the couch. She'd insisted on praying over lunch and included her usual requests for a cat and a mommy.

While the little girl slept, Callie checked her emails. One of the agents from the office messaged her and asked her to meet at a house in

Burlington to do a walk-through. Happy to have something to do, Callie replied she was free the next day. How she'd bill Mr. Martin for it, she didn't know, but at least she knew how to write an invoice. They still needed her, she knew, and they were going to pay for it.

Callie gritted her teeth with determination, and a little light bulb went off in her head. If she could stage houses as a freelancer, there was no reason she couldn't stage houses for other realty companies.

Of course. She was an independent contractor now, or she could be. If she staged houses for several real estate offices at once, she could make more than she'd been making to start with. She'd already referred several agents in the area to Mark. She should have offered her own services, too.

"You have to think like an entrepreneur sometimes, not just a designer," she said out loud. Quickly running a search on real estate companies south of Atlanta, it was hard for her not to let the creative side take over and start looking at how to build a website. She'd just have to work faster and harder. She could do it. In no time, she could save enough for a down payment on a shop.

Mr. Martin letting her go could very well be a blessing in disguise. She didn't need to go back to Nashville, and more than ever now, she had every reason to stay.

Excited and pleased, she started jotting down notes on paper scraps. Her box of notebooks was still in the back of the car where'd she tossed it after moving her personal things out of the office. She hurried out to get it, stacking tools leftover from the farmhouse in her arms and tottering into the house. She dropped office supplies onto the floor beside the couch and carried the chalk paint and brushes into the kitchen.

Pulling the brushes out, she made sure they were dry and set them on the edge of the sink. She started to put the box of paint in the cabinet underneath, but the little silver spoon she'd found in the hutch clattered around, and she stopped. She didn't want it ruined if it got damp under the sink. She'd forgotten all about it.

Callie pulled the spoon out and admired it. It looked unique and very old. She'd meant to show it to Mark a couple of times but kept forgetting. Flipping it around in her hand, she tried polishing it with the hem of her T-shirt. It didn't help much. It was definitely ancient.

She walked back to the couch and set it on her lap while she searched for antique spoons online.

A picture popped up on the screen, and Callie scrolled through several images of single pieces of silver that had gone for top dollar. She raised a brow. A New York auction house had sold a few sets of Irish silver in recent years. She looked down at the spoon again and turned it over. This looked like a quality piece. On a hunch, she clicked an image of Irish silver. Her heart began to thump. She'd never realized it was so rare and valuable.

With nervous hands, she searched for more Irish designs, then almost choked when she saw the same maker's mark as the one on the spoon in her lap. She looked at the price point and became light-headed. Irish silver, so old and rare that no one had entire collections anymore, was worth a fortune. Collectors searched and bought up individual pieces hoping to make complete sets.

Callie stopped on a picture of a fork with the same design as her little spoon. For a moment, she couldn't breathe. Croaking out a laugh of disbelief, she picked up the almost three-centuries-old spoon and held it against the screen. She couldn't believe it. She was holding twenty thousand dollars in her hand.

Chapter Fourteen

Mark drove around the block in Atlanta's midtown twice before he accepted the fact that he would have to pay for parking. With a brick of dread in his chest, he heaved himself out of the truck and carried the box of spoons toward the auction house, wishing there was some other way. Once again, his prayers hadn't been answered, and he would just have to bite the bullet.

A pleasant-sounding bell chimed as he passed into a cool, dimly lit foyer. It was nice. Posh. Not a place he fit in wearing work slacks and a checkered Oxford. The elderly woman at the reception desk offered him a drink when he checked in, but he declined. She smiled and asked him to sit down while she picked up the phone. He walked to the other side of the sitting area, too nervous to sit but needing to get away from her strong perfume.

Examining the fine art on the wall, he jumped when someone said, "Mr. Chatham?"

Rodney Bennet, his contact, strode up to him with his hand out. They shook hands, and Bennet motioned for him to follow. "Let's go to my office."

Mark nodded and went along like an obedient schoolboy. It felt dreadful to be standing here with his mother's precious heirlooms, all just to save his shop's space on the town square to sell junk. But there was the house, he reminded himself, and the land. He'd just have to pick and choose. This wasn't about him anymore, it was about Hadley.

The knowledge that he had no choice didn't make him feel any better or less guilty. He'd let them all down. He'd let his entire family down. He said a prayer that his mother would forgive him for parting with the spoons.

His throat felt like someone was squeezing it, and Mark took a sharp breath as they walked into Bennet's nice office. The worst part was, if he fell behind again, he'd have nothing left but the land. He hoped Bennet would be generous.

The man took a seat behind his desk. He looked Mark in the eye instead of gawking at the box. "I'm sorry you're in the situation you're in."

Mark nodded.

"This isn't the way I wanted to buy your spoons from you, but I promise I'll be fair."

Mark cleared his throat. "I appreciate that. I knew you would, and that's why I drove up this far."

Bennet leaned forward. "Are they still in mint condition?"

"They are." Mark set the small box on the floor in front of him and opened it up. Callie had lovingly wrapped each piece in lint-free cloth and stacked them in neat rows two deep. He picked up three and set them on the desk.

Bennet unwrapped the first one and held it up to the light. "Beautiful," he murmured. He slid a desk drawer open with one hand and pulled out a magnifying glass. His eye became enormous as he examined the spoon from one end to the other.

He set the magnifying glass down and smiled at Mark. "If the rest of them are as good as this, I can offer you forty-five hundred for the set."

He hadn't been expecting to get so close to market value. Mark took a deep breath. "That's more than generous," he said in a hushed tone.

"Well, I think I'm going to hang on to them," Bennet admitted. "They increase in value every year right now, and they have such a great story."

"The Harts from Rhode Island." Mark nodded. Bennet didn't know the half of it. True love, sacrifice and a hero coming home again.

"Can I see the rest?"

The remaining spoons were unwrapped and examined, and twenty minutes later, Bennet pushed back from his desk. "It looks like we have a deal." The phone on his desk buzzed, but he politely ignored it. He stood up and stuck out his hand, and with a defeated cloud pressing down on him, Mark forced himself to stand, too. At least the store was saved.

The phone buzzed again, and a rapid patter of footfalls and a frantic series of raps on the office door interrupted them. Mark raised a brow at all of the commotion.

Bennet looked embarrassed. He pivoted around the desk and strode to the door. Someone banged on it again, and it burst open just as he reached for the handle.

Callie burst into the room, her hair a windblown mess and still wearing a pink T-shirt over a pair of jeans ripped at the knee. Hadley came panting in behind her. She looked confused but excited. Callie was beautiful.

Mark stared, and she burst into laughter when she saw him. "Stop," she said with a wide smile and watery eyes. "Don't do it."

Bennet looked confused. He swung his gaze back to Mark.

"Callie?" Mark didn't know what else to say.

She brushed past Bennet and practically jumped into Mark's arms. She looked deep into his eyes. "Don't sell the spoons."

He blinked.

She turned to Bennet. "I have something better for you."

The dealer looked irritated now. He walked back to the desk, brows low, and looked to Mark for some kind of explanation.

He had nothing. Mark looked at Callie.

"Mr. Chatham will not be selling his spoons today," she announced in an authoritative voice.

"Excuse me?" Bennet's cheeks turned red. He clamped his mouth back together in a grim line.

Callie dropped into the chair Mark had been sitting in and held out her fist. It looked like she had a plastic bag.

"What is this?" Bennet said. The annoyance in his tone sounded barely contained.

"Irish silver." Callie flashed him one of her whopping grins. "A rare and valuable piece." Even as Mark saw her set the plastic bag down on the desk, he couldn't help but admire the deep dimple in her cheek. For whatever reason she was ruining his business deal, she was doing it adorably.

Bennet snatched up the bag, pulled out a small tarnished spoon and stared at it. He glanced up at Mark, then back at the spoon. Picking up his magnifying glass he turned the spoon over, and Mark watched the color empty from his face.

Mark turned to Callie. "Whose is that?"

"It's not mine," Hadley reassured him.

Callie waved at Mark to hush him up and kept her dazzling eyes locked on Bennet's. "It's ours. We're partners."

"Partners," Hadley parroted.

Bennet looked at Mark for confirmation, and he nodded before Callie looked back at him. He had no idea what she was up to or what she had, but the excitement in the room was palpable.

The art dealer set the magnifying glass down. "Do you have proof of ownership?"

"I can get an affidavit," Callie said confidently. "The spoon was sold years ago to Mr. Chatham at auction along with a 1941 walnut china hutch, which he sold to me." She looked back and gave Mark a reassuring nod. "I held on to the receipt," she added for his benefit.

"You never turned in your receipt?" Mark said out loud, and blessed her absentminded heart for not getting compensation from Martin Realty for the hutch.

She shook her head. "The hutch is mine," she assured him. She waited for Bennet to set down the spoon. It was all Mark could do not to snatch it away from him so he could see it himself.

"That's a rare seventeenth-century Irish silver spoon, Mr. Bennet," Callie said, "and I'm sure you saw the maker's mark."

Bennet eyed her. Mark's spoons wrapped up in their lint-free cloth on the desk had been forgotten.

"I'll offer you fifteen thousand," the dealer said in a firm voice, and Mark's jaw dropped.

Callie raised a brow. "I've already notified the auction houses in New York, and I'm sure you'll be contacting them as soon as you buy this." She smiled, then in a serious tone added, "Eighteen thousand, firm, and we'll need an advance today while you have it authenticated."

Bennet took a deep breath and exhaled. He was focused on Callie now; Mark was a shadow. "I can counter all day, but I see you're one step ahead of me."

She nodded. "We need the cash," she admitted, "and we have no emotional ties to the piece."

Bennet made a noise in his throat and looked at Mark. "I suppose you've changed your mind about these?" He glanced down at the family spoons.

Mark looked at Callie.

"Yes," she answered for him, "he has."

He moved close beside the chair and rested his

hand on the back of her neck. "Yes," he repeated, "I've changed my mind. I'm sorry, Bennet."

The older man looked disappointed but said, "I understand, but I can't complain about the substitute." He held up the Irish spoon again. "Young lady, do you have any idea what you've found?"

Callie looked up at Mark. "I have a pretty good idea."

His heart leaped. Without thinking, Mark pulled her up by the elbow and drew her into his arms. It didn't matter that Bennet was there. It didn't matter that he didn't understand what was going on between them. Mark gazed into her eyes.

"The spoon was in the hutch," she whispered, "behind the drawer." She chuckled. "It would have never been found if we hadn't decided to bring the hutch back to life and give it a second chance." She gave him a tight squeeze. "Tell the bank that you'll have the money on Monday."

A tidal wave of relief washed over Mark, from his head down to his toes, making him go weak in the knees. His heart swelled with joy, gratitude and mad, mad love for this woman. "You did this for me."

"I did. All for you—and a little girl. And if I'm lucky, you'll let me buy into the Market and tell Martin Hometown Realty to jump into the lake."

He would have laughed, but he had to kiss her, so he did. She melted in his arms. This time, no one had the nerve to interrupt them. Not even Hadley.

Epilogue

The for-sale sign in front of the old Pierce farm-house came down. Callie squealed with excitement as she burst through the front door. Mark followed, laughing right behind her. He tossed the placard down onto the couch while Callie danced around.

"You did it!" She hopped up and down, then dashed into his arms. He gave her a long, tight squeeze until she looked up.

"I couldn't have done this without you," he whispered. His husky voice and sincere gaze made her heart melt.

"You did this," she assured him. "I think it's brilliant to rent out your house. I mean, your other house. Now the land can be farmed, and it's not all on you, but it's still in the family."

"Right," he agreed. He loosened his grip around her waist and spun her around in a slow dance. "With the shop renovations done and all of your pieces moving so fast…" he winked "…I'll have more than enough time to keep this place up."

"Hadley will love it here. She's already picked out her room!" Callie grinned. "And I'm happy to do my share. I love being part owner of the Antique Boutique. My mother would have been proud."

He chuckled. "You just like the new name."

She shook her head, her heart swelling with happiness. "No, I love the store and the building. I told you McIntyre would sell it to you in exchange for your little lot across the street from the house. A new subdivision means more to him than a little old junk shop on the block, as he called it."

"I'm glad you were right." Mark smiled. "I wasn't so sure."

"He had no choice," Callie said loftily. "It was either losing a little building on the square or missing out on making millions with his new neighborhood."

Mark pulled her down onto the couch. "I can't believe he gave up something that's been in his family for generations."

Callie gave him another squeeze.

"So what do you think of me moving all the

way out here by myself with my little girl?" he asked. "Are you going to miss me?"

Callie decided to tease him. She put a finger to her chin and pretended to think. "Well, it is a long drive," she sighed, "but the lake is nearby." She beamed at him. "I think I'll manage."

He closed his eyes. "I'm glad to hear that," he whispered, then he blinked and sat up. "They'll be coming for the staging furniture," he told her, and she realized he was right. He motioned toward the kitchen. "We should get the hutch moved out of the way before they get here since it's still yours."

"Ours," she corrected him. She could never think of the hutch as hers now. In a way, it'd brought them together. It had led her back to him and made her dreams come true. "I can't believe I'm out of debt now and part owner of an antiques shop," she said, sidetracked from their mission. She giggled and kissed him on the cheek. "I'm keeping that hutch forever."

"Oh, yeah?" He cocked his head at her. "Maybe we should keep it here then."

"Oh, okay," Callie said. She tried to hide the windfall of disappointment she felt. She'd hoped he would help her move it to her house. She'd extended her rental agreement on the cottage another quarter. "I guess it does look perfect where it's sitting in the kitchen," she added in a small voice.

Mark took her hand and pulled her up. "Let's go have a look."

She followed him to the kitchen, trying not to drag her feet. She didn't want to squabble over the hutch, but his sudden change of heart had taken the wind out of her sails. They stopped beside the dining table and studied it.

"It is sweet," she admitted, admiring her work. She swallowed down a lump in her throat. "To think how many generations passed down that spoon until it got lost behind a drawer."

Mark nodded, sharing in her disbelief. "Are you sure you found them all?"

Callie laughed and elbowed him. He looked serious, though. "Maybe you should look again."

Callie snorted. She walked over and pulled a drawer open. "Empty," she said. She looked back at him and gave a teasing shrug. "I guess your mother's spoons will just have to go in here."

"Check the other one," he insisted.

She stared at him for a second, unsure if he was serious or not. She turned back to the hutch and pulled the second drawer open. It was empty, except for a navy blue velvet jewelry box.

Callie's heart sped up. Behind her, Mark became still. The entire house seemed to hold its breath. She forced herself to reach for the gift box and pull it out, not sure how to act and not certain what to expect. Her heart thudded so hard it echoed in her ears.

Turning around with it in her hand, she met Mark's steady gaze.

"Open it, Callie," he whispered.

She looked down and opened the lid. It snapped up on its tight hinges. Time seemed to stand still. An inexplicable sob rose in her throat and tears blurred her vision, but she could still see. She blinked them away. The stunning oval-cut diamond was set in antique rose gold.

She raised her eyes to Mark. He looked paralyzed, then he took a sudden breath like he'd forgotten how to breathe.

"Old and new," he said in a hushed voice. "My mother's wedding band and the first diamond I saw that reminded me of you."

The tears spilled down her cheeks. Callie put a hand over her mouth to keep from sobbing.

He finally crossed the room to her. "I don't want to live out here in this farmhouse alone. And my little girl, she's quit praying for the cat. She just wants you. We both do."

Callie laughed and sobbed at the same time. The man! He knew she loved him and his daughter. And this house. She adored it—

wanted it—but couldn't afford it or keep it up on her own. She gazed into his gray-blue eyes and believed what she saw there. He'd bought it for her.

"And I want kids," he added. His cheeks flushed. "Our own little boy or girl to take to the softball field." A smile escaped. "Hadley wants a baby brother."

Swallowing to keep from hiccuping, Callie closed her eyes and pressed her forehead to his. "This is better than an entire set of Irish spoons," she said, then broke into a happy, nervous giggle.

Mark grinned and held on to her hands as he slipped down to one knee. He swallowed audibly, and her heart went out to him. She knew he felt awkward. It was hard for him to find the words sometimes.

"I love you," she blurted, and he beamed up at her.

"I love you, too, Callie Hargrove." He glanced past her at the hutch, then looked into her eyes again. "I know I'm a few years late, but won't you marry me?"

She pulled him to his feet and jumped into his arms again. "Of course, I will, Mark Chatham," she said, squeezing him tight. "For good and forever. Your daughter's prayers are answered."

He chuckled under his breath, then took her chin in his hand.

"Now let's talk about where we're going to hang our spoons," she teased.

He threw his head back and laughed, a rare, delightful sound, then took her by the waist and kissed the smirk right off of her face.

* * * * *

*If you enjoyed this book,
be sure to check out these other titles*

The Black Sheep's Salvation *by Deb Kastner.*
Home to Heal *by Lois Richer.*
A Father's Promise *by Mindy Obenhaus.*
The Cowboy's Missing Memory
by Shannon Vannatter.

Available now from Love Inspired!

*Find more great reads at
www.LoveInspired.com*

Dear Reader,

Thank you for visiting Ragland, Georgia, and cheering for Mark and Callie. I love the South—the landscapes and cultures have long been a part of my life—and I believe it's the perfect setting for heartwarming romances where family and friends are as important as barbecue, grits and sweet iced tea. I hope you felt a touch of that in Ragland and feel the same way.

Once torn between pursuing success in the big city or a simpler life down gravel roads lined with Queen Anne's lace, I can relate to Callie's dilemma in sorting through her dreams and where they should take her. But with age comes wisdom, and I've learned that happiness and love come from within us and not outside ourselves.

Then there's Mark. He represents what I admire most in men—sensible, hardworking, gentle, honest and passionate about what he believes in and wants most. Best of all, he loves his little girl with everything he has. Good daddies empower young women, and empowered women change the world.

Special thanks to my Georgia friends, mother, sister and dear husband, who suffered through my regional road trips searching for history and inspiration.

Thank you to Melissa Endlich and Harlequin Love Inspired for giving me the opportunity to share Callie and Mark's story and helping me make it all it could be. Thank you to my readers and friends who laugh, cry and cheer with me day after day and shape my world and writing.

I can easily be found on Facebook, Instagram and Twitter. Feel free to connect, discover more of my books or share your thoughts on *His Daughter's Prayer*.

My best wishes to you and yours,
Danielle